Everyone Else's Parents Said Yes

PAULA DANZIGER

Delacorte Press

Published by
Delacorte Press
Bantam Doubleday Dell Publishing Group, Inc.
666 Fifth Avenue
New York, New York 10103

Design by Richard Oriolo

Library of Congress Cataloging in Publication Data
Danziger, Paula, [date of birth]
     Everyone else's parents said yes / by Paula Danziger.
          p.   cm.
     Summary: Matthew cannot resist the temptation to play
practical jokes on his older sister and all the girls in his class at
school, so by the time of the big party for his eleventh birthday
they have all declared war on him.
     ISBN 0-385-29805-6
     [1. Schools—Fiction.   2. Family life—Fiction.]   I. Title.
PZ7.D2394Ev   1989
[Fic]—dc19   88-37540
                                                                    CIP
                                                                    AC

Manufactured in the United States of America
October 1989
10 9 8 7 6 5 4 3 2 1
BG

TO FRAN AND JULES DAVIDS,
with a lifetime of love

Acknowledgments

Patricia Reilly Giff—*for support and "noodging"*

The Danzigers—*Barry, Annette, Sam, Carrie, Ben, and Josh*

The Stantons—*Betty, Frank, David, Paul, and Bryan*

The Kids All Over the Country Who Have Shared Their Ideas, Experiences, and Suggestions

Everyone Else's Parents Said Yes

Chapter 1

"Mom. You know there are only five more days, fifteen hours, and thirty-two minutes until my birthday party." Matthew Martin enters the kitchen holding a computer printout.

Matthew Martin can be very organized and accurate when he wants to be, and he wants to be. Since he's the youngest person in his sixth-grade class, birthdays really count.

"I know, honey. One hour ago you came in here and told me that there were only five more days, *sixteen* hours, and thirty-two minutes until your birthday party." Mrs. Martin can also be very organized and accurate, even while she is busy following the recipe for zucchini-carob-chip bread.

"Listen to him. You'd think that no one ever had an eleventh birthday before." Amanda Martin applies polish to her very bitten-down nails and wrinkles her nose at her brother. "I didn't make a big fuss about it two years ago when I had my eleventh birthday. You're such a big baby."

"Two years ago, you did make a major fuss about it." Mrs. Martin grins, reminding her. "Nothing would do but to take twelve girls to Adornable You, the store where you make things to decorate yourself."

Matthew offers, "I'll get the picture out of the scrapbook to prove it. You and those goofy girls wearing"—pausing, he puts his hand on his hip and acts like a model—"all those silly feather things and ugly sparkly jewelry. Goofy, goofy girls. Yuck."

"Shut up, runt." Amanda glares at him.

"I'm not a runt. Just a little short for my age. Daddy says he was like that, too, and now look at how tall he is!" Matthew shouts at her. "And look at you, runt chest, who do you think you are?"

Mrs. Martin sighs. "Amanda, stop calling your brother a runt, and, Matthew, don't refer to your sister's chest as a runt chest. In fact, don't refer to your sister's chest at all."

Amanda and Matthew can tell that their mother is trying not to grin.

Amanda stands up and yells, "It's not funny! He's disgusting. I hate him. And you make it worse by laughing at what he says. Why did he ever have to be born? Why did I?"

"She always acts like the big shot she isn't." Matthew sticks his tongue out at her.

She stomps out of the room.

Mrs. Martin puts her hand on her head, leaving zucchini batter on her forehead. "Children. I should have gotten goldfish as pets instead."

"Then you could have had a pool party for the goldfishes' birthday." Matthew licks the cake beaters.

Wiping the batter off her forehead, Mrs. Martin says, "Very funny. Now, Matthew, I want you to stop teasing your sister so much. She's just entering adolescence, actually stomping her way into it, and it's not going to be an easy time for her. Not for her . . . not for me . . . not for any of us, I have a feeling."

"I was born to drive her nuts," Matthew informs her. "And we both know that's not going to be a long trip."

"Matthew." His mother has a way of saying the name so that it takes forever and means stop being a wise guy.

"Oh, okay, Mom." Matthew puts down the cake beaters. "Now, about the party, you said I should think about it. Well, I've decided. I want a sleep-over in the backyard."

"Okay. Remember, your father and I work hard and we need your help with the party." Mrs. Martin smiles.

"Right." Matthew shows her the computer printout in his hands. "Don't worry. I've got everything under control. Here are the lists."

Mrs. Martin pours the batter into a pan, puts the pan

THE KIDS

BILLY KELLERMAN
TYLER WHITE
JOSHUA JACKSON
BRIAN BRUNO
DAVID COHEN
PATRICK RYAN
MARK ELLISON
PABLO MARTINEZ

THE FOOD

HOT DOGS

HAMBURGERS

POTATO CHIPS

SODA

CAKE

ICE CREAM

ALL THE JUNK FOOD
IN THE WORLD

THINGS TO DO

GET PRESENTS

OPEN PRESENTS

HAVE COMPUTER NINTENDO TOURNAMENTS

GIVE OUT PRIZES TO TOURNAMENT WINNERS

EAT

ALL OF US MAKE FUN OF AMANDA AT ONCE

TELL JOKES

GIVE OUT PRIZES FOR BEST JOKES

GO TO SLEEP

WAKE UP

EAT

ALL OF US MAKE FUN OF HOW AMANDA
LOOKS IN THE MORNING

EVERYONE GOES HOME

PLAY WITH MY PRESENTS

into the oven, sets the timer, washes and dries her hands, and finally sits down to look over Matthew's lists.

* * *

"I think that you are going to have to reexamine your lists." Matthew's mother smiles. "The guest list is fine, but there are a few items in the other lists that will have to go."

"Okay. So we won't go to sleep." Matthew grins at her.

"That's not it, kiddo." She pats him on the head. "You will leave your sister out of this."

"That's all I ever want to do. Leave my sister out of everything, my life, the house . . ." Matthew sticks his fingers into the leftover zucchini batter and then licks them.

"Matthew."

"Oh, okay. I'll take all of the stuff about her off the list. Then will everything else be okay?"

Another "Matthew."

"Yes." He grins, knowing what she's going to say.

"I really feel that you should reconsider all that awful junk food on your list and make some healthy substitutions—carob candy, fruit rolls, things like that."

"Come on, Mom. Everyone else's parents let them eat junk food."

Mrs. Martin sighs. "Matthew Martin. How many times must I tell you that we're not everyone else's parents? If everyone else's parents let them jump off the roof, should we let you jump off the roof?"

"It's just a little junk food, not nuclear destruction," Matthew pleads.

"I'm not sure that there's much difference between eating junk food and nuclear destruction." Mrs. Martin shakes her head.

Matthew sometimes wishes that his mother were more like his best friend's, Joshua Jackson's, mother, who says things like "Isn't Granola a Latin American country?" and "Tofu, isn't that the crud under your toenails?"

"Mom, please. Look, the guys will hate me if we serve the stuff you like. They call *that* stuff junk food, and even Dad likes real junk food. . . . And anyway, everyone else's . . ." Matthew stops himself from repeating his favorite phrase.

Mrs. Martin sighs again. "This is against my better judgment, but all right. You may have some junk food at your party. It's a losing battle with you sometimes, but I'm telling you right now, I'm going to make a very healthy cake."

"Oh, okay." Matthew tries to look sad, as if he's giving in, but deep down inside he feels like he's won the Super Bowl of Handling Mothers. He actually got his mother to agree to some junk food!

It was going to be a great party, no doubt about it.

Chapter 2

"Hey, want to trade desserts?" Matthew stares at the contents of Joshua Jackson's lunch box.

"Are you kidding? Your mom makes you eat healthy junk."

Joshua takes out a package of three cupcakes, which are filled with cream and covered with marshmallow and coconut icing.

"Please, I'll be your best friend if you share those with me." Matthew holds back a drool.

"You already are my best friend." Joshua starts taking the cellophane off the cupcakes.

"Umm. Look at this." Matthew holds up his dessert.

"What is it?" Joshua makes a face.

"Whole-wheat-fruit slices. Yummy. I'd be willing to give up four of them, all four of them, for just one of your three cupcakes. What a deal!" Matthew holds up the Baggie as if he's holding up a trophy.

"No deal." Joshua licks the top of one of the cupcakes and then takes a bite out of it.

"I'll be your best *best* friend," Matthew pleads.

"You said that last week. What was that mess I traded a cupcake for?"

"Cottage-cheese-yogurt cake," Matthew reminds him. "Oh, Joshua. This is better. Come on. Please. I can't help it if my mother makes me eat this stuff."

Joshua looks at his remaining two cupcakes and then at his best friend. "Here's the deal. I give you the cupcake. You don't give me the fruit slices."

"Fair deal." Matthew reaches for a cupcake.

"Not yet." Joshua stops Matthew's hand in mid-grab. "You have to help me learn how to play Defender Dragons better."

Defender Dragons. Matthew's best computer game, the one where he racks up the highest scores of anyone in the class, of anyone in the entire school.

Matthew looks at his friend, then at the cupcake, and back to his friend. The cupcake. The friend. "All right, not all of my maneuvers, but enough to get you to the next level. How about that?"

"It's a deal." Joshua hands over a cupcake and thinks that with the kind of stuff Matthew's mother cooks, he's going to be able to learn how to get to all of the levels.

As Matthew puts the cupcake into his mouth he tries

to eat it slowly, tasting every little bit, licking the icing, eating the cake, saving the cream center until the end.

It's too late. Something in Matthew acts like a vacuum cleaner, sucking up the cupcake in what seems like seconds.

Looking down at the whole-wheat-fruit slices, Matthew thinks of how his parents are always telling him not to waste food, to think of the poor starving people in the world.

Mr. Farley, the head lunchroom monitor, goes up to the microphone, taps it, and yells into it, "ALL RIGHT, YOU KIDS! It's time to go out to the playground. Don't forget the rules. Make sure all garbage is put in the cans, go out quietly, no pushing or shoving, and if anyone has spilled milk or food, notify us immediately so that no one gets hurt."

Mr. Farley has been very worried about spilling since the time he rushed over to stop a fight between two sixth-grade boys and he slipped on milk and banana.

He broke his foot and used crutches for a long time to walk and once to separate the same two sixth-grade boys who were fighting again.

Everyone rushes out.

Mr. Farley steps back.

Matthew gets into line to throw out his garbage.

Lizzie Doran is in front of him.

Stepping on the back of her sneakers, he says, "Oops, so sorry."

She turns around. "I know you're not sorry. Matthew Martin, you are so immature."

"Thank you." Matthew loves to annoy Lizzie.

"You're not welcome." She turns her back and ignores him.

Matthew smiles.

School gets boring sometimes, he thinks. It's fun to do stuff like this.

Matthew throws out his garbage, holding on to his dessert, which he places under a tree outside, thinking that maybe some poor starving birds would like to eat it.

As he looks down at the whole-wheat-fruit slices, he thinks that the birds won't like them either, that they would prefer worms, that he would probably prefer worms if he were a bird.

"Keepaway! Sixth-grade boys over here to play Keepaway," Brian Bruno is yelling.

Joshua and Matthew run over to where Brian is standing with the ball and start running away from it as fast as they can.

Matthew is beaned by Tyler White.

As Matthew stands on the sidelines and watches, he is glad that Tyler White is no good at Defender Dragons.

Looking around the playground, Matthew checks on what everyone is doing. The sixth-graders are hogging all the best spaces, like they always do. At Elizabeth Englebert Elementary, where the cheer "Go E.E.E." sounds like pigs squealing, the sixth-graders get dibs on practically everything.

Matthew has waited a long time for his class to reach the sixth grade. The next big event for him will be becoming a teenager.

Matthew thinks about his upcoming birthday and how he's getting closer.

Looking at the sixth-grade girls, who are also playing

Keepaway but at the other side of the playground, Matthew thinks about how it was back in the old days at E.E.E. when they all played together, not just in gym class.

Something had changed and now it was all different.

Matthew remembers how he spent the first few weeks getting used to the school's new computer graphics program and teaching all the boys how to make fancy signs for their doors that said ALL GIRLS, KEEP OUT. THIS MEANS YOU.

It amazed Matthew that not all of the boys were interested in making that sign, that some of them even wanted to make others, especially Patrick Ryan, who made one that said ALL GIRLS, ENTER. THIS MEANS YOU.

Mark Ellison is out next, yelling, "No fair!"

Mark Ellison always thinks it isn't fair when he loses.

Then Patrick Ryan is out. He walks away, making jokes as if he doesn't care, but he does. Patrick Ryan plays to win.

Soon it is down to Joshua against Tyler White.

Tyler throws the ball at Joshua's head, but Joshua ducks, grabs the ball, and throws it at Tyler, hitting him on the rear end.

Everyone cheers and gives high fives to Joshua.

Heads you lose, tails I win, thinks Matthew as the bell rings, signaling back-to-class time.

Usually Matthew hates that bell, but not today.

Today he's going to ask Mrs. Stanton for time to do his party invitations using the new computer graphics program.

He can hardly wait.

Chapter 3

"We sent out two gorillas in tutus, one six-foot-tall, pink singing chicken, four tap-dancing birthday cakes, a teddy bear on roller skates, and a grandmother who delivers chicken soup." Mrs. Martin hands the plate of broccoli to Mr. Martin. "And that was just the early part of today."

Mr. Martin is interested in his wife's new job at the place that sends out people in costumes to deliver singing telegrams, gifts, balloon-o-grams, and other surprises for special occasions. "What about later in the day?"

"It was a disaster. There were only two major jobs—a birthday party for a six-year-old and a fiftieth wedding anniversary. Mickey Mouse and Minnie Mouse were supposed to tap-dance a birthday song to the kid, and a man in a tuxedo was supposed to deliver a dozen roses to the couple. Did that happen? No. It did not."

Waiting for a minute to build up the suspense, Mrs. Martin shrugs.

Matthew, trying to find a good place to hide the broccoli, asks, "What happened?"

"Mrs. Grimbell, the owner, made a mistake and confused the orders. She seems a little distracted. Anyway, the guy in the tuxedo delivered the roses to the boy, who kept saying, 'Where are my helium balloons? I wanted us to inhale them and make our voices change,' and the couple could not quite believe that there, in their own living room, were Mickey and Minnie tap-dancing 'Happy Anniversary to You' and throwing confetti all over the place."

"What did the old folks say?" Matthew chops up his broccoli and puts it under the rim of his plate.

"The woman kept saying, 'Look at this mess. Are you planning to vacuum it up?' and the husband said, 'Helium balloons. Great. We can inhale them and listen to our voices.'" Mrs. Martin laughs.

"It sounds much more exciting than my day," Mr. Martin says. "Want to trade? I'll take your job and you can be a lawyer."

"Nope." Mrs. Martin shakes her head. "I like what I'm doing. However, maybe you can help out. There's a chance that tomorrow I will be one person short. Would you be willing to put on a gorilla suit and go to an engagement party wearing a sign that says MELVIN GOES APE OVER GINA?"

"I'd love to." Mr. Martin nods. "And then I can wear the gorilla suit in court. That way the people who believe that there's a lot of 'monkey business' going on in court will think that they have proof."

"Daddy. Don't. I'd die if anyone saw you dressed as a gorilla," Amanda whines. "And, Mom, why can't you get a normal job like other mothers? You do this just to embarrass me. Everyone's asking if you do strip grams."

"Not me personally." Mrs. Martin acts horrified. "And, Amanda, your father and I are just kidding around. He's not going to get dressed in costumes."

"Shucks." Mr. Martin looks sad. "You have all the fun. You get to dress up in costumes."

"Only if it's an emergency. That's not my regular job," Mrs. Martin reminds them.

"Mom. Promise you won't wear costumes. I would die!" Amanda begs and threatens.

Mrs. Martin shrugs. "A woman's got to do what a woman's got to do."

Deciding to change the subject, Mrs. Martin holds up the plate. "Anybody want seconds of the tuna-tofu casserole?"

"No thanks." Matthew shakes his head, waves the plate away, and wonders what Joshua is eating tonight.

"No thanks, honey." Mr. Martin looks down at his half-full plate and remembers the great meal he had at lunch. "So, kids, how was your day?"

"Great."

"Terrible."

Both responses come out at the same time.

16

"Which of you would like to go first?" Mr. Martin asks.

"He might as well, since his day was so wonderful and mine wasn't." Amanda bites her nails.

"Honey, stop biting your nails." Mrs. Martin reaches for Amanda's hand.

Amanda pulls her hand away.

Matthew decides to ignore Amanda and speak. "Mrs. Stanton gave me permission to work on my party invitations using the new program, and I've decided what to put in the goody bags, and everyone I'm inviting is going to be able to come to the sleep-over."

"What do you need the invitations for then?" Amanda asks.

Matthew continues to ignore Amanda. "And I've got a great idea for the design of the invitation and the graphics and the colors."

"I really should upgrade our machine," Mr. Martin thinks out loud.

Amanda jabs at her tofu-tuna. "Doesn't anyone care about my day? All he's talking about is making up invitations for the party to send to people who already know about it and have already said that they're coming. How dumb can you get?"

"Amanda." Mrs. Martin makes the name sound five times as long.

"Well, it's true. And here I sit with my life in a shambles, and it's all your fault." Amanda's lower lip moves forward.

"Why is it our fault?" Mr. Martin asks.

"Today, Bobby Fenton called me 'four eyes.'"

Well, she is, Matthew thinks, annoyed at being

interrupted. The four F's: Four-eyed, Flat, Funny-look-
ing, and Fingernail-stubbed.

He bites his lip to keep from saying it out loud. No
reason to take a chance on getting grounded just before
his party.

Amanda starts to cry. "It's all your fault. If only you'd
let me get contact lenses. . . ."

"No. We've been through this already. Dr. Sugarman
says to wait a little bit longer. By next year you can get
them."

"Next year." Amanda sighs. "Everyone else's parents
let them get contact lenses this year."

Not true, Matthew thinks, knowing at least six of her
classmates who wear glasses.

"We're not everyone else's parents," her mother says.
"We're your parents and we say that you must wait for
the lenses until the doctor thinks it's right."

"A year." Amanda makes a face. "Well, at least let me
have plastic surgery then."

"What!" her parents yell at the same time.

"For my ears. One is lower than the other and my
glasses are crooked. If my ears were even, the glasses
wouldn't be tilted."

Everyone looks at Amanda's face.

Everyone thinks her glasses look perfectly fine.

Mr. and Mrs. Martin think her face looks perfectly
fine.

Matthew thinks she should have plastic surgery on her
entire face.

"Amanda. Be reasonable. Dr. Sugarman said that there
was a slight difference in your ears, that many people
have that problem, and that all it takes is to adjust the

glasses a little. He did that. There's no problem. You are very pretty," her father says.

"You're my father. You have to say that." A tear rolls down Amanda's face.

Matthew cannot understand what she's making such a big deal about and hopes that he doesn't turn weird when he becomes a teenager.

He also thinks about how long it will be before she goes away to college and he has the house and his parents to himself. Too long. Not soon enough.

Tomorrow wouldn't be soon enough, let alone five years.

While Amanda continues, Matthew tunes out and thinks about the contents of the goody bag that each person at the party will get—M&M's, a box of raisins, sweet tarts, wax teeth with fangs, a packet of baseball cards with bubble gum, and one of those licorice rolls with a candy center. He's happy with the choices—junk food with one healthy thing, the raisins, to make his mother a little happier. To make himself a little happier, he would have added about eight other candies, but his parents and the budget that they gave him wouldn't allow it.

He tunes back in to what's happening.

Amanda is still talking. "And it's all your fault that I have to wear glasses. If you two didn't have bad eyes, I wouldn't."

Matthew thinks, Maybe she should blame it on their grandparents. They had to wear glasses too. Maybe she should blame it on the dinosaurs. They probably caused cavemen to squint from looking up at them. Then the cavemen needed glasses and it was passed on to future generations.

Amanda doesn't quit. "And it's not fair. Look at that little twerp. He doesn't have to wear glasses."

"That's because they like me better than they like you," Matthew teases. "And my ears aren't even lopsided."

Matthew has trouble stopping once he starts. "And I'm not ugly, and dumb, and acting like a turkey."

Amanda stands up. "You repulsive little runt."

"Enough!" Mrs. Martin yells.

"To your rooms. Both of you," Mr. Martin orders.

"It's not my fault!" Amanda and Matthew yell at the same time.

"Well, it's definitely not our fault," their father says. "I want you to go to your rooms and think about what you've done."

Both kids go off to their rooms, mumbling, "It's not fair. It's not my fault."

Matthew goes to his room and thinks about what he's done. Nothing.

It's Amanda's fault.

It always is.

Someday, he thinks, *some*day, I'm going to get even.

Chapter **4**

"Matthew. That's not very nice." Mrs. Stanton looks over his shoulder. "And I don't think that you've really followed the assignment."

"Why not?" Matthew, with an ink mark on his nose, looks up at her. "You said that we should make up a greeting card using words and numbers. Well, I did."

"That's not a very nice greeting," Mrs. Stanton tells him.

"It's for my sister. She's not a very nice person so she doesn't deserve a very nice greeting card. The only greet-

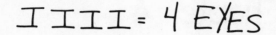

Roses are red,
Violets are perkle.
Amanda Martin is a four-eyed jerkle.

ing she ever gives me is 'Get out of my way, nerd face.' "

"Matthew. When your sister was in my class she was very nice. I know that brothers and sisters don't always get along." Mrs. Stanton speaks softly. "But your sister is really very nice. Someday I'm sure that you will realize it."

Matthew says, "I'm never going to like my sister. She's turned into a monster. We're never going to get along, ever. Not now. Not when we're ninety."

"Well, I hope that you aren't always going to feel that way, and, Matthew, you really shouldn't call people names. It's not right to call someone 'four eyes.' "

Matthew realizes that Mrs. Stanton is wearing glasses. He's not sure what to say.

She continues, "And you shouldn't call her a jerk."

He knows what to say about that. "I didn't. I called her a jerkle. That's a word that I made up. It means 'dear, sweet, wonderful sister.' "

He can tell by the look on Mrs. Stanton's face that she doesn't believe him.

He wouldn't believe himself either if he were the teacher.

Mrs. Stanton sighs. "Start over, Matthew. Throw that card away and start over."

Matthew pleads, "Do I have to?"

"Yes." Mrs. Stanton means business.

"I'll do a card for my mother and I'll throw this one away later," he promises, knowing that there is no way that he wants to throw out the card to Amanda.

"It's your choice, Matthew. Throw that card away now and be able to use the computer later for your invitations, or hold on to the card and not be able to use the computer later for your invitations."

"Aw." Matthew knows when he's beaten. "I'll throw the card out now."

"Good boy," Mrs. Stanton says.

Matthew goes up to the wastepaper basket, puts the card in, and thinks about how he's going to make another card when he gets home.

Jill Hudson calls out, "Ow, Ow, Ow!" She keeps waving her hand.

Jill Hudson finds it impossible to just hold up her hand and wait until she gets called on by a teacher. She has had this habit since kindergarten.

"Yes, Jill." Mrs. Stanton calls on her.

"Can I make an announcement to the class? Ow, Ow, Ow. It's very important." Jill is practically jumping out of her chair.

"Very important?" Mrs. Stanton doesn't sound so sure.

"Ow. Ow. It is! It is!"

"All right." Mrs. Stanton looks as if she's not too sure that she's making the right decision.

Jill announces, "I've decided that my name is very boring."

"So are you!" Brian calls out, and then pretends to yawn.

All of the boys start pretending to yawn.

Jill ignores them. "Everyone else has nice names, like Cathy, who can also be called Cath or Catherine. Lizzie can be Liz or Elizabeth. Ryma, whose mother promised to name her after her Grandmother Mary but made the name nice and different. Lisa Levine, whose names go well together. Vanessa. Jessica. Zoe and Chloe, who have beautiful names if people don't make them sound like they rhyme with toe." Jill stands up at her desk. "You know, if they make them rhyme with Joey—"

"Jill, please get to the point." Mrs. Stanton is grinning and shaking her head.

"I am. I am. Katie can be Kate or Katherine or Kath, and Sarah's name is just so pretty."

"The point, Jill. You've named all of the girls in the class, so get to the point." Mrs. Stanton looks up at the clock on the wall. "It's almost time for recess."

Jill gets to the point.

Jill is not the kind of person who likes to be late for recess.

"I've decided to make my name more exciting. I can't change it to Jilly, because the dumb boys will make it rhyme with Silly."

"And Pilly and Dilly," Tyler calls out.

"Billy and Jilly sitting in a tree.
K-I-S-S-I-N-G."

"Shut up, Tyler!" Billy Kellerman yells out. "I'm going to get you for that."

"Children." Mrs. Stanton uses her "very teacher" tone.

Jill ignores all of the fuss. "So I've decided that from now on my name will be spelled Jil!, with an explanation point at the end to make it more exciting."

"ExCLAMation point." Mrs. Stanton grins.

"Whatever." Jill, now Jil!, goes on, "And when you say my name make it very dramatic, because that's what the explana—because that's what that mark means."

"Ow! Ow! Ow!" Pablo waves his hand, doing a Jil!

25

imitation. "Mrs. Stanton, I think that it should be Jil? with a question mark instead. To show that it isn't easy to understand how Jil? got so weird."

The bell rings for recess.

Mrs. Stanton excuses the class.

The students, except for Matthew, rush outside.

Matthew sits down at the computer, prepares a new disk, and begins.

It's going to be the best invitation ever.

Chapter 5

Computers.

Cakes.

Stars with elevens in them.

A tent.

All the important information.

It had taken Matthew the entire recess and lunch period to finish, but it was worth it.

Everyone would know that Matthew Martin was the best in computer design.

He did the work himself.

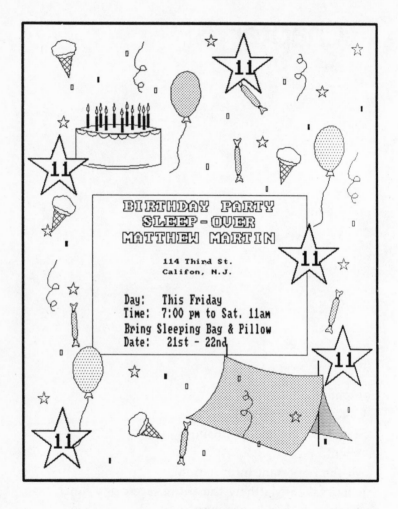

BIRTHDAY PARTY
SLEEP-OVER
MATTHEW MARTIN

114 Third St.
Califon, N.J.

Day: This Friday
Time: 7:00 pm to Sat. 11am
Bring Sleeping Bag & Pillow
Date: 21st - 22nd

No program for him.

He was the best.

No one could beat him at Computer.

David Cohen was better at remembering the planets and elements.

Katie Delaney always won the spelling bees. In fact, practically everyone in the class was a better speller than Matthew.

Joshua and Tyler were great athletes.

Brian Bruno was already a brown belt in karate.

Best artist was Mark Ellison.

All the girls thought that Patrick Ryan was "the cutest."

Matthew doesn't care about cute. He doesn't think much about what he looks like. He knows that he has straight brown hair that never looks combed even when it is, because Amanda is always saying things like "Doofus. You should use hair conditioner on that mess." Amanda also says, "Your eyes look like they could use a pooper scooper." It's not the brown eyes that bother Matthew, but the freckles drive him nuts. His grandmother always pinches his cheeks and says, "My darling little freckle face." Matthew knows that he doesn't look like Frankenstein, Dracula, or Freddy from *Nightmare on Elm Street*. What he doesn't know is what makes a girl think that someone's cute, and actually he doesn't care that he doesn't know.

What he does care about are computers, and no one could ever say that Matthew Martin wasn't the best at Computer, especially after they see the invitations.

Matthew continues work on the invitation, adding little details, while the rest of the class comes running in.

"Hey, Matthew. You missed it. I got six baskets."
Joshua pretends to still be dribbling the ball.

"Great." Matthew doesn't look up.

"Matthew. It was really fantastic. You should have been there." Joshua tries to get his friend's attention.

Matthew still doesn't look up.

"That's it." Joshua is getting annoyed. "Stop with that stupid machine already. Or else."

Looking up, Matthew sees that Joshua is holding on to the computer cord.

"Don't fool around with that!" Matthew yells.

In the background he can hear Tyler singing "Billy and Jilly sitting in a tree."

"Stop that," Billy yells, "or you're going to be sorry. Very sorry!"

Before Joshua can put down the computer cord, Billy pushes Tyler, who bumps into Joshua, who accidentally pulls the plug out of the extension.

It's all over for the invitation, which Matthew had not yet stored.

Matthew stares at the now-darkened computer monitor.

Joshua comes over and looks at the screen. "I'm sorry. I didn't mean to. It was an accident."

The rest of the class comes into the room.

Mrs. Stanton, who comes in last, takes one look at the room and rushes up to pull Billy off Tyler, who is lying facedown on the floor.

"It was an accident. I slipped." Billy tries to look innocent.

"Sit down." Mrs. Stanton points to a chair.

"Are you all right?" She helps Tyler get up and hands him a tissue for his bloody nose.

"Gross." Chloe looks at the blood coming down Tyler's face.

Matthew continues to stare at the darkened monitor.

"Everyone sit down while I take care of this," Mrs. Stanton says.

"I'm sorry," Joshua repeats, tugging on Matthew's sweatshirt. "Come on. Say something."

Matthew looks at the screen where four minutes earlier had been something that he had been planning for weeks and had worked on for most of the day, the free-time part of the day.

It was all gone.

"Joshua. Go to your seat," Mrs. Stanton calls out. "Now."

"Say something," Joshua says, before heading for his seat. "Say something."

Matthew glares at him and whispers, "I hate you. I don't want you to come to my party. I don't want you to be my friend."

"Well, if you feel that way about it, who cares? You act so dumb sometimes." Joshua turns and goes to his seat.

"Matthew. Back to your seat too. You can finish that invitation later." Mrs. Stanton walks with Tyler to the door. "Tyler, go to the nurse, and then I want you to go to the principal's office and explain what happened."

Billy Kellerman is smiling because Tyler has to go to the principal.

"You may go there right now, William Kellerman," Mrs. Stanton says.

Billy Kellerman stops smiling and gets up.

Matthew Martin is sitting at his desk and feeling rotten.

Chapter 6

Today has to be one of the worst days of Matthew's life.

Three whole days without speaking to Joshua . . . and today Joshua was really disgusting.

Joshua Jackson, his best friend, his ex-best friend, brought in bags and boxes of junk food for everyone, everyone except his best friend, his ex-best friend, Matthew Martin.

It must have cost him two months' allowance. There were jujubes, Sugar Babies, gum drops, chocolate Necco wafers, Cheetos, sour cream and onion Ruffles potato chips, circus peanuts, Snickers, Gummy Bears, Worms, and Dinosaurs, Reese's peanut butter cups, and M&M's, plain and peanut. It was torture.

Passing the junk out at lunch to all of the sixth-graders, except for his ex-best friend, Joshua ignored Matthew except to say, "Enjoying your rice cakes with unsweetened jelly, turkey?"

"If you want more," Joshua informed everyone, "you better not give any to Matthew."

It was terrible.

Lizzie Doran refused to take any because it was mean what Joshua was doing to Matthew, even though it was true that Matthew sometimes drove her nuts.

Matthew decided that Lizzie Doran was okay and that he would never again do things to bug her.

Brian Bruno snuck one brown M&M to Matthew.

Then, at Keepaway, Matthew was not only the first person out, but he was out because he got slammed by Joshua.

Before, Joshua had never aimed for Matthew. It was always someone else who had gotten him out.

In school Matthew noticed that Joshua was having trouble with one of the computer programs.

When Joshua said, "Could someone give me a hand with this?" Matthew pretended to be engrossed in a math problem.

After school, the time when the two boys usually hung out together, each went home alone, even though they lived down the street from each other.

Both acted as if it didn't matter, as if they were invisible to each other.

Now Matthew was home and there was more trouble.

"Kids. Your mother has to work late and I don't want to miss bowling tonight. It's the first round of the tournament," Mr. Martin tells his children.

Matthew is rummaging through the refrigerator, hoping that one of the carrot sticks had magically turned into a lemon meringue pie.

Amanda is in the kitchen only because she has been called downstairs for this discussion.

Most of the time she stays in her room, pouting about being contact lens-less, about not being able to have plastic surgery on her ears, and about not being able to have a private phone in her room.

Mr. Martin continues, "Now, listen. I've tried to get a baby-sitter."

"I don't need one," Amanda informs him. "Kids my age are baby-sitting already."

"That's what I want to talk to you about," Mr. Martin says. "I want you to baby-sit for us today."

"I'm not a baby. I don't need a sitter!" Matthew yells. "And definitely not her."

"Are you going to pay me?" Amanda is thinking about the possibility of saving up to have her own private phone installed.

"Are you going to pay *me*?" Matthew is thinking about how he deserves combat pay for putting up with his sister.

Mr. Martin shakes his head. "You two are impossible. You should be happy to help out, to be part of the family. The only reason for a baby-sitter is that your mother and I won't be home until very late and we don't think it's safe to leave the two of you at home alone, without a referee. However, we can't seem to locate one for tonight. They are probably all officiating at wrestling matches and hockey games instead of realizing that we would need them to watch our children."

"That's because you won't leave junk food for them, the baby-sitters, I mean. They're all sick of the stuff in our refrigerator," Amanda informs them.

Matthew is not surprised by this piece of information. However, his father is. "Honey, that's not true. We've always tipped very well and no one has ever complained."

"It's in the unwritten baby-sitters' code not to complain to the parents. But it is true. I know it is. There's a kid in my class, Sharlene, and her older sister, Darlene, baby-sits a lot. Darlene told Sharlene that there's a list that baby-sitters share with each other grading all of their jobs. In the food category, we got a G."

"What's a G?" Mr. Martin is getting a headache.

"It's like the school grades, where we get A, B, C, D, or F. We didn't even rate an F. We were below Failure." Amanda sighs. "It's so hard being part of this family."

Standing up, Mr. Martin holds up his hands to signal STOP. "I've got to get going. Now I want you to be in charge, Amanda. I will pay you."

"No fair!" Matthew yells. "I'm in sixth grade. You treat me like such a baby. No one else's parents get a baby-sitter."

"Be good and I'll pay you too," Mr. Martin offers. "I can't believe it. I'm offering my children bribes to act like human beings. It's against everything I believe in and I'm doing it anyway."

"I'm in charge, right?" Amanda asks her father.

"Right. Don't abuse the authority." Mr. Martin picks up his bowling ball and heads out the door.

Amanda grins evilly at her younger brother.

Matthew's day keeps getting worse and worse.

It's not even fun thinking about his upcoming birthday party anymore.

Amanda goes to the phone.

For the next two hours she is on the phone talking to her girlfriends.

Stupid girlfriends, Matthew thinks. Stupid Amanda.

It's no fair. She's going to get paid to be on the phone all night, which is something she's not allowed to do when their parents are home.

Matthew sits in his room, thinking that if he and Joshua were still friends, he could have gone over to the Jackson house and not had stupid Amanda in charge. Or Joshua could have come to the Martin house and they could have ganged up on Amanda by making rude noises into the extension while she was talking to her stupid friends. It was harder to do stuff like that alone. It was more fun to gang up on her together with Joshua. She had more trouble trying to catch both of them at once.

This being mad at Joshua was no fun.

But Joshua deserved it.

Matthew only hoped that Joshua was just as miserable.

Chapter 7

"Open the door, nerd face. I want to talk to you." Amanda pounds on the door.

Matthew yells, "Stay away, baboon breath!"

Amanda is silent for a minute and then knocks on the door again.

"Go away." Matthew is in a bad enough mood already without having his sister come in and play boss.

"Honey baby, I really have to talk to you," Amanda pleads.

Matthew can't believe that she's calling him "Honey

baby." She hasn't done that since they were little and he actually believed that she was going to be nice to him. He was too smart for that now.

"Honey baby." Amanda opens the door and sticks her head in the door.

Matthew pretends that she is invisible.

In the old days it was never safe when she said "Honey baby" so nicely. Once she did it when she was eight and he was six and she decided to give him a "new look." She cut his hair all spiky, with a pinking shears, and then sprayed his hair bright pink. It took months for it to grow back, and he was the only kid in the first grade whose mother had to dye his hair every couple of weeks. And then there was the time in second grade when she conned him out of every cent in his Fred Flintstone dinobank so that she could get her ears pierced after their parents had told her she couldn't. They made the holes close up by not letting her put earrings in. She never repaid him, and when he complained to their parents, they said it was his fault for lending her money for something that she wasn't supposed to do.

When Matthew was little, he was very gullible when it came to his sister. Now he knew better.

"Honey baby." Amanda comes into his room and stands by his bed, looking so sweet.

"No," Matthew says. "No. No. No. Absolutely not."

"But I haven't even asked you for anything yet. How do you know that I want anything?"

"NO. NO. NO." Matthew sticks his fingers in his ears.

Amanda tries a different method of getting to her brother. "Listen, pea brain. I want you to help me."

Now Matthew feels better. They are on familiar

ground. He's used to dealing with his sister this way. He doesn't feel as defenseless with name-calling as he does when she's doing her "Honey baby" routine.

"It's going to cost you." Matthew stares at her. "You're going to have to give me part of the money you're going to get for baby-sitting me."

Amanda says, "No fair. You're getting paid too."

"Fair? You're my sister. Who says I have to be fair to you? You never are to me." Matthew isn't sure what they are fighting about, but it doesn't matter.

"Please," Amanda pleads, looking so sad that Matthew feels sorry for her.

"Oh, okay. I'll listen. But don't expect me to say yes."

Amanda sits down on the edge of his bed and then jumps up because she has just sat on his Invaders of the Universe rocket ship. "Matthew, can't you ever be neat?"

"It's my room," he reminds her.

This time she checks before she sits down. "Matthew, I want you to do me a favor. Could you please watch yourself for about half an hour?"

"You want me to stand in front of a mirror and look at myself for half an hour?" Matthew grins at her. "I don't know, Amanda, that could be very tiring."

"You goof brain," Amanda says, forgetting for a second that she's trying to get him to do something for her.

"Goof brains don't do favors for sisters." Matthew is having fun for the first time all day.

"Honey baby, please." Amanda really begins to beg. "I just want to go over to Cindy's house for half an hour. It's very important."

Cindy is Joshua's older sister. Cindy's house . . . that's Joshua's house too.

Matthew thinks, Maybe I should say yes, it's okay. And then I should wire Amanda with a bomb that will go off when she gets over there. That would solve a lot of my problems. . . .

Matthew thinks about it for a minute and knows that that is too awful and disgusting a thing to do, even to Amanda and Joshua.

"Please," Amanda begs.

"Why?" Matthew wants the details.

"Because," Amanda tells him.

"Tell me." Matthew knows he's got his sister exactly where he wants her.

"Oh, okay," she relents. "I'll tell you. But you've got to promise not to tease me or anything."

"I promise." Matthew is not sure if he will keep the promise. After all, it is only to his sister.

"You better." Amanda glares at him, forgetting for a second that she really wants something from him. "This Friday is very special."

"I know. It's my birthday party," Matthew says.

"No," she says. "Really special. You have a birthday every year. That's not so special."

Matthew gets ready to tell her why it's very special, but she doesn't give him the chance.

"Really special. There's a school dance . . . and Danny Cohen asked me to go with him."

Danny Cohen. That's David's stepbrother. . . . David, who is in my class. Matthew thinks, I hear that Danny's really a nice guy. Why does he want to go out with my sister? I wonder if insanity runs in his family. I better ask David tomorrow.

"And I have to go over to Cindy's house to try on some clothes so I have something to wear on Friday. I have nothing to wear."

"Nothing to wear." Matthew picks up the rocket ship and pretends to be dive-bombing at her head. "Nothing to wear! You have so many clothes that they don't fit into your closet. You have to use the hall closet too."

"I have nothing *new* to wear. Nothing special. I'm going to wear something of Cindy's and she's going to wear something of mine. That way it'll be like we've each got new clothes." Amanda sighs. "I don't know why I'm trying to explain this to you. You don't even care about clothes. You're the kid who went away to camp and never changed your underwear for an entire week."

"That was a long time ago," Matthew tells her.

"Yeah. Last summer." Amanda pushes her glasses back on the bridge of her nose.

"You can go over to Cindy's house," Matthew tells her. "It's going to cost you though. Half of whatever you make tonight baby-sitting."

"One fourth," Amanda bargains. "I've decided to spend it on a new pair of shoes. Real high heels. And I won't have enough money if I have to give half of it to you."

"Half. Take it or leave it."

Amanda looks at her watch and realizes that the longer it takes to compromise, the less time she'll have at the Jacksons'. "Okay, okay," she relents. "And you promise not to tell our parents."

"Promise." Matthew thinks about how he can use the

baby-sitting money to buy more stuff for the goody bags . . . that he'll use it to buy Almond Joys, Joshua's favorite. Then he remembers that he and Joshua are no longer friends.

"Thanks, Matthew. I really appreciate this." Amanda sounds like a normal person. "And, Matthew, one more thing . . ."

Matthew grins. Another favor. It's going to cost her.

"Matthew," Amanda continues, "Cindy and I were talking—"

"I know. That's all you two ever do," Matthew teases her. "Yak. Yak. Yak."

"Shut up and listen for a minute. Cindy and I were talking about you and Joshua and the fight. She said that Joshua is really unhappy about it, and I can tell that you are too."

"Am not." Matthew shakes his head and folds his arms across his chest.

"You are too. I can tell." Amanda pushes her glasses up again. "Cindy told me what happened. It really did sound like an accident. You and Joshua have been friends for too long to act like this to each other. I remember when Cindy and I had a fight in sixth grade. It was really dumb. Look, I'm older than you are. I have more experience in stuff like this. Listen to me. It was only a dumb invitation."

"I worked on it for hours. It was the best invitation ever."

"Matthew. I know that computers are important to you and how good you are on them. You're better than almost anyone I know. But it's also important to have friends. You can't play ball outside with a computer or

42

have a real-friends type of talk with a computer. A computer can't share junk food with you." Amanda looks at her watch. "I've got to go. Think about what I said. Your dumb birthday party is important to you. Are you going to ruin it by not having your best friend there? That'll turn this whole thing into a big deal."

"Why are you telling me this?"

"You're my brother." She shrugs. "Sometimes, weird as it seems, I even like you. Look, I've got to go. Promise that if our parents get back, you'll call and warn me."

"I promise." Matthew nods.

"Bye." Amanda jumps off the bed and rushes off.

"One more thing, turkey!" Matthew calls out.

"Yes?" Amanda stops.

"Keep all of the stupid baby-sitting money. You can buy your stupid high heels. Even though you'll probably break your stupid neck wearing them." Matthew can hardly believe that he is saying this.

Amanda comes back, gives him a kiss on the forehead, and then rushes out.

Matthew wipes the kiss off his forehead and wonders if he's been possessed by a devil who is making him so generous.

Then he thinks about what Amanda said.

Maybe she's right.

Maybe she isn't.

Maybe he will talk to Joshua tomorrow.

Maybe he won't.

Whoever said that being a kid was easy never had a best friend, or a sister, and would never be invited to Matthew's birthday party, not ever.

Chapter 8

"That breakfast is really gross." Amanda looks down at her brother's plate. "How can you eat granola with catsup?"

"Easy." Matthew grins. "With a spoon."

"Ha, ha." Amanda looks up at her brother. "You wouldn't be able to do that if Mom and Dad were here."

"But they aren't. You know that they both had to go to work early. And Mom made me promise to eat the granola. I really hate it. I really like catsup. I'd rather mix it with vanilla ice cream and chocolate syrup, but since we can have that stuff only on special occasions, I put catsup on it." Matthew puts some in his mouth. "Friday, I will actually be able to have some ice cream, syrup, and cake BECAUSE—"

"I know. I know! Because it's going to be your birthday." Amanda makes herself some whole-wheat toast. "Really, Matthew. I can't understand why you're making such a big deal out of your birthday. After all, everybody has them."

Matthew swirls the granola-catsup mixture with his spoon. "It's important. It's the one day a year when people really make a fuss over a kid. When everyone has to be nice to you, and you get a lot of presents that you could never buy for yourself. And in this family it's one of the few times we can have junk food. When you're a kid it's practically the biggest day of the year, except for Christmas, maybe. Did you buy me a present, Amanda?"

She looks at him. "You are so greedy."

"Yes." He grins. "So what did you get me?"

"I'm not telling." She puts grape jelly on her toast.

"So you did buy me a present." Matthew claps his hands. "Tell me what it is."

"Matthew. Stop it." Amanda pulls her brother's hair. "Stop being a pest. And hurry up, you're going to be late for school. Mom made me promise that I would be sure to get you out of here on time."

Matthew stares down at the breakfast that he has hardly eaten.

"Get going. And thanks for not squealing on me. I owe you one." Amanda puts the toast into her mouth.

"Good." Matthew tries to get her to pay up immediately. "If you owe me one, would you please eat my breakfast for me?"

Amanda looks down at the granola-catsup mixture and says, "Not a chance. I'd barf."

Matthew picks up the bowl. "I have an idea."

"Just don't be late for school or you're going to be dead meat." Amanda shakes her finger at him. "I have to go to school now. Cindy and I are getting to school early. We have to talk."

Matthew thinks about all of the talking they did yesterday, first on the phone and then in person, and thinks about how much girls gab. He was sure that Danny Cohen and whatever sucker was taking Cindy to the dance were not spending all this time talking about what they were going to wear and junk like that.

Amanda leaves.

Matthew looks down at his breakfast and knows that when his mother comes home, she's going to check the garbage to see if he ate the granola.

He thinks of flushing it down the toilet, but knows that he can't. The last time he tried that the five-grain eggplant soufflé stuffed up the toilet. So no toilet stuffing allowed.

Putting the breakfast in a Baggie, he takes it and his books and lunch outside. He grabs a shovel out of the garage and buries the breakfast Baggie under a bush in the front yard.

He debates burying his spelling book, too, but realizes that's not a good idea.

Matthew is so intent on burying the evidence that he doesn't realize that Joshua is standing behind him watching the whole thing.

"Ashes to ashes. Dust to dust." Matthew remembers what he saw on a television show once. "The next thing I'll bury is whole-wheat crust."

"That is so lame." Joshua starts to laugh.

Matthew looks at his friend and stands up. "Hi," he says quietly.

Both boys just look at each other and then both say "I'm sorry" at the same time.

Then Joshua punches Matthew on his arm, not a fight punch but a friend punch.

Matthew does the same to Joshua.

The fight is over.

"We better get to school," Matthew says, grabbing his books and lunch. "We don't want detention. We have to plan for the party."

"Okay. Race you." Joshua starts to run.

I'll never keep up, Matthew thinks, but Joshua doesn't run as fast as he can, so the two boys run side by side.

"I brought an extra pack of cupcakes today." Joshua holds up his lunch bag. "You can have them unless your mom packed you something better."

The thought of the cupcakes makes Matthew sprint even faster. "She packed tofu-sunflower-seed brownies. Even though it's going to be a sacrifice, I'll give them up for the cupcakes."

As they near the school playground Matthew thinks about something they'd learned in school, about how Indians used to pass the peace pipe when they wanted a war to end.

With Matthew and Joshua, it was peace cupcakes instead.

The Surgeon General would probably approve.

Matthew was glad the fight was over . . . with or without the cupcakes.

Planning the party was going to be fun again.

Chapter 9

"I'm in deep trouble, deep, deep trouble," Brian Bruno informs the guys. "I'm not sure that I'm ever going to be allowed out of my house ever again, except for school and church."

"What did you do?" Mark asks.

Brian starts to grin. "You know my little sister, Fritzie the Pain?"

Everyone knew Fritzie. Before she learned to talk she learned to bite. Each boy had at least one scar on his leg to remind him of Fritzie. Four years younger than Brian, Fritzie was a real pain . . . in a real way.

Brian continues, "You know how she's always follow-ing us around, butting in?"

Everyone nods.

"Well, I decided to get even. So I trained her," Brian tells them.

"Trained her not to bite? Trained her to give herself a rabies shot?" says Patrick Ryan, looking down at his an-kle, where there is still a Fritzie scar.

"No such luck." Brian shakes his head. "No, I trained her to do something else. Every time I would say 'Who am I?' she would have to say 'King Brian, the terrific.' And then I would say 'Who are you?' and she would say 'Fang face, pig brain, Fritzie.' "

"Great," says Mark. "I'll have to teach that to my little sister."

"No way." Brian shakes his head. "My parents heard us and they got mad, told me that I was the oldest and should know better, that I was being mean and had to be punished."

"Oh, no. You can't come to my party." Matthew, who knows how Fritzie must feel being the youngest, still sides with Brian.

"I begged them. I got down on my knees and pleaded with them to let me go," Brian says. "I promised them if I could go, I'd give Fritzie my goody bag, that I'd take her to the movies two times without complaining, that I would never call her 'fang face' again."

"What happened next?" Matthew needs to know.

"I apologized to the little snaggle-toothed creep in front of my parents and they said that I could go to the party, that my grounding wouldn't start until after the sleep-over, and then the punishment would start. So no one have a party for the next month, okay?"

Matthew thinks about how hard it is for brothers and sisters to get along, about the time he dropped water balloons on Amanda's head and she screamed, "I will not use force on you. I will use verbal!" Sisters sure are strange.

Mrs. Stanton walks into the room. "Class, everyone sit down quietly."

Trouble, Matthew thinks. I have a feeling that there is something I have not done.

Once everyone is seated, Mrs. Stanton says, "Who would like to hand out the paper?"

"Ow, Ow, Ow," Jil! is practically jumping over the top of her desk, frantically waving her hand.

Mrs. Stanton turns to the quietest child in the class. "Ryma. Please pass out the papers."

Once the papers are on everyone's desk, Mrs. Stanton says, "Number from one to twenty."

The spelling test! Matthew remembers, but he remembers too late to do anything about it.

Ten minutes later everyone puts his or her pencil down on the desk.

Matthew's paper is a mess. It's so erased that there are holes in the paper. There are cross-outs. Smudge marks. It looks like it's been in the hands of a dirty demento.

"Exchange papers with the person to the right of you," Mrs. Stanton tells them.

Matthew groans. He has to give his to Vanessa Singer. She hasn't liked him since the time he put the class gerbil in her Barbie lunch box. It's not that he expects her to cheat for him. He just hopes that she doesn't scream out his grade. Maybe she'll be nice.

No such luck.

"Has anyone else gotten fifteen wrong . . . or did Matthew win the Spelling Booby Prize again?" she yells out.

"Vanessa. That isn't very nice." Mrs. Stanton looks at her. "How would you feel if someone did that to you?"

Vanessa sticks her nose up in the air and shakes her curly red hair. "There's no way that could happen to me. I would never get that many spelling words wrong. Never."

Matthew wants to murder her.

He also wants to die of embarrassment.

It's not fair.

Why is spelling so important?

His computer program beeps and changes wrong spellings, so why are they bothering with these stupid spelling tests anyway?

Finally, the agony ends and the class has independent reading time.

Matthew pretends to read but actually thinks of ways to get even with Vanessa.

He can feel something start to rumble inside his body.

He debates asking for the bathroom pass but decides against it.

Instead, he sits at his desk and expels gas in Vanessa's direction, one of those SBD's, Silent But Deadly. Then he immediately holds his nose and calls out, "Oh, yuck. Vanessa. How could you do that? You're so disgusting."

Everyone in the class turns around and looks at Vanessa.

"I didn't do anything. You did, you disgusting pig."
Vanessa is blushing.

Matthew puts on his most innocent look, his most
hurt look. "Me? Why don't you just confess? I'm sure it
was an accident. Don't be so ashamed."

Everyone near them starts moaning and holding their
noses.

Vanessa gets redder and redder.

Matthew is having a great time.

Vanessa looks like she's going to cry.

Matthew feels a little bit guilty until he remembers
how she told everyone what a dope he was in spelling.

This will teach her.

Matthew may not be the world's best speller, but he
has just made everyone think that Vanessa is the world's
worst smeller.

Next time Vanessa will think twice before she messes
with me, Matthew thinks.

Little does he know that Vanessa is already plotting
her revenge.

Chapter 10

Matthew feels like he's struck gold. He's got the black-mail evidence of the century!

Going through Amanda's school notebook to get some paper, he has found the list.

Mrs. Stanton had said that he had to write each mis-spelled word ten times.

Ten times fifteen words. That's going to take a lot of paper.

Mrs. Stanton had warned him.

He is not to do it using his computer, writing it once and having the computer repeat it fourteen more times.

He did that last time.

This time she says that if he does it again, he's going to have to handwrite each word twenty-five times.

Twenty-five times fifteen is more than Matthew cares to compute.

So he was prepared to write it out, using cursive.

However, he's left his notebook at school.

Going into the kitchen to look for paper, he has found Amanda's notebook.

Amanda Martin Cohen
Amanda Cohen
Mrs. Amanda Cohen
Mrs. Danny Cohen
Ms. Amanda Martin
Mandy Cohen
Mrs. Amanda Martin-Cohen
Mandy Martin
Mandy Martin Cohen
Amanda M. Cohen

a. Martin Cohen
Mrs. Daniel Cohen
Mr. and Mrs. Danny Cohen
Mr. and Mrs. Daniel Cohen
Mrs. and Mr. Dan Cohen

It's like striking gold.

He can really blackmail her with this.

He's sure that she'd be willing to write fifteen spelling words ten times each rather than have anyone see what she's been doing.

Matthew is sure that all he is going to have to do is threaten her with giving the paper to David Cohen, who will then give it to his stepbrother, Danny.

Amanda walks into the room just as he begins to pull the page out of the notebook.

"What are you doing, you little runt?"

Matthew holds up the page. "Wait until Danny sees this!"

Amanda rushes toward Matthew, backing him against the refrigerator.

He ducks under her arm.

Sometimes being a runt has advantages.

However, he ducks right into his father, who is behind Amanda.

Getting his son into a headlock, Mr. Martin says, "Hi, boy. What's going on?"

"Nothing," Matthew says. "How about letting me go, Dad? I have some spelling homework to do."

"Kill him!" Amanda screams. "Break his stupid little runt neck! He stole something very important of mine."

Mr. Martin, who does not believe in physical violence, shakes his head.

The hold on Matthew is not strong, but Matthew knows better than to try to break away.

"Drop it." Amanda sounds ready to do serious harm.

Matthew grins at her. "Mrs. . . ."

"Shut up." She pulls his hair.

"Let go," Mr. Martin says. "Matthew. You let go of your sister's paper. Amanda. You let go of your brother's hair."

Matthew lets go of the paper.

Amanda lets go of his hair.

Mr. Martin lets go of Matthew.

"Now what's going on here?" Mr. Martin wants to know.

Matthew knows that if Amanda squeals, he's going to be in trouble. He also knows that if Amanda squeals, he's going to have to tell about her leaving the house the other night while she was supposed to be baby-sitting.

Amanda knows that if she squeals on Matthew, he's going to squeal on her.

"It's all right, Dad. I'm not going to press charges." Amanda has been watching *People's Court*.

"Are you sure?" Mr. Martin asks.

"I'm sure," Amanda sighs.

Mr. Martin looks down at his son. "Matthew. I'm not sure what you were up to, but I have a feeling that you were up to no good. Watch your step, son."

Matthew knows that he's going to need his father's help in setting up the tent for the sleep-over, so he uses his most innocent look and says, "Yes, sir."

Mr. Martin, remembering how he and his sister always used to fight when they were little, looks at his two children. He only hopes that someday they will learn to get along just the way he and his sister, their Aunt Nancy, now get along.

Matthew looks at Amanda.

It doesn't look like she's too happy with him.

However, he decides to press his luck.

"Can I borrow some paper from you? I need it to do my homework," Matthew asks.

Amanda debates stepping on his head, but then looks at her father, who senses that she wants to step on Matthew's head and is going to make sure that doesn't happen.

"Oh, okay. What do you need?" She opens her notebook, careful that only empty pages are showing.

"Five pages," he tells her.

"Spelling words again." She shoves the paper at him. "Next time, ask first."

"Okay." Matthew takes the paper and leaves.

Amanda looks at her father. "He's such a child."

Mr. Martin remembers that it was only a week ago that his daughter said "It's no fair. I'm only a kid" when she was asked to help clean up the house.

Amanda sits down on the kitchen stool. "Daddy, can't you help me convince Mom that I need contact lenses?"

"No way." Her father shakes his head.

"Plastic surgery?" she persists.

His head shakes again.

"For my date with Danny, can I have him meet me at Cindy's house? It's going to be awful having him meet me here with that stupid party going on. Matthew is going to do something terrible to embarrass me. I know he will. Please, Daddy? Oh please." Amanda puts her head down on the kitchen table.

"Get up, honey." Mr. Martin runs his hand over the back of her head.

"Not until you help me with this problem." Amanda is hard to hear because she is talking into the table.

Mr. Martin thinks for a minute and then says, "Your mother and I want Danny to come here. You can't deprive us of seeing you go out on your first date. However, I do know that there is a chance that Matthew may try to do something embarrassing."

Mr. Martin is remembering his sister's first date and how he rigged up the stereo system so that, as they walked out of the door, "Here Comes the Bride" played loudly enough for the whole neighborhood to hear it.

"I'll talk to him, warn him, I promise," Mr. Martin tells her.

Amanda raises her head. "Thanks, Dad."

Getting up, she gives her father a hug.

As she leaves the room she says, "Tell him if he's not good, we're going to give all of his presents away. That should do it."

Mr. Martin says, "I'll take care of it."

Amanda walks upstairs and heads directly to Matthew's room. "Listen, you little brat, if you ever tell anyone about that page, you are dead meat."

Matthew smiles at her.

"I'm not kidding." She stares at him. "If you do any-

59

thing when Danny picks me up, I'm going to tell everyone how, when you're upset, you still sleep with your
Babar stuffed elephant, the one you got when you were a
baby."

"I don't and you know it." Matthew stands up.

"You know that and I know that, but no one else will.
They'll believe me and think you are a nerd to the nth
degree." Amanda grins evilly.

Amanda knows she's got Matthew, that the kids will
tease him even if it's not true. She also knows that she'd
really never do that to him, but he doesn't know that.

As Amanda leaves the room, Matthew sits down
again.

What a day.

One hundred and fifty spelling words to write.

Amanda's threatening to turn him into the class geek.

And somewhere out there Vanessa Singer is planning
her revenge.

Chapter 11

We, the girls of Grade Six of E.E.E., do hereby form an organization called GET HIM, which is short for Girls Eager To Halt Immature Matthew.

We plan to do everything possible to make Matthew Martin's life as miserable as he has made ours.

SO MATTHEW MARTIN, WATCH OUT!!!!!!!!!!!!!!!!!!!!!!!!!!!!!!!!

THE GET HIM EXPLANATION:

Just so people don't think that we are being unfair gang—ing up on Matthew Martin, fink of Califon, fink of New Jersey, fink of the United States. North America. Earth. The Universe. Matthew Martin, slimeball of all eternity, we do hereby list just a few of the sneaky, disgusting, and rotten things that he has done to us!

1. Putting catsup and mayonnaise in his mouth, puffing up his cheeks, smacking them to make the goop come out of his face onto Cathy Atwood's brand—new dress, and screaming, "I'm a zit! I'm a zit!"

2. Always making fun of Jessica Weeks's last name, saying dumb things like "Jessica Weeks makes many daze." And whenever he sees her with her parents and little sister, yelling out, "Look! It's the Month family——Four Weeks equals one month." Enough is enough!

3. Rolling up rubber cement into tiny balls, labeling them "snot balls," and putting them into Lisa Levine's pencil box.

4. Ever since preschool, kicking the bottom of the chair of the person who is unlucky enough to be seated in front of him.

5. Whenever anyone taller stands up in front of him, yelling, "I can't see through you. What do you think, that your father's a glazier?" We can't help it if practically everyone in the class is taller than Matthew. It's especially mean when he does it to Katie Delaney. She can't help it if she's the tallest person in the class.

6. Putting a "Sushi for Sale" sign in the class aquarium.

7. Teasing any boy who wants to talk to one of the girls, acting as if it were the crime of the century. Just wait until Matthew gets old enough and acts more mature (if that ever happens, especially since he is the baby of the class) and wants to ask some girl out on a date. No one in this class is ever ever going to go out with him. We've made a solemn promise as part of GET HIM. He's going to have to ask out some girl who is presently in preschool or not even born yet because we have also made a solemn promise to inform every girl in the world to WATCH OUT!

8. During the Spring Concert quietly singing the theme song from that ancient TV show Mr. Ed while everyone else was trying to sing the correct songs.

9. Putting Bubble Yum in Zoe Alexander's very very long blond hair, so that her mother had to spend four hours rubbing ice cubes on it, and then, when told about what a pain it was, said, "I guess that helped you cool off, you hot-head."

62

10. On last year's class trip to the Bronx Zoo, going up to the attendants, pointing to all the girls, and saying that they had escaped from the monkey cages.

11. Bothering all the girls at lunchtime to make them trade their meals for the sprouty stuff he always brings.

12. Always acting like such a bigshot about computer stuff, never helping out any girl who needs help, and acting like Chloe Fulton doesn't exist because she's almost as good as he is at it and could be even better if she didn't have so many other interests. SO THERE!

13. For the Valentine Box, giving the girls envelopes filled with night crawlers. Even though it was anonymous, we all know who did it. Even if Mrs. Stanton said we couldn't prove it, we know it was Matthew because most of the names were spelled wrong. So was the handwritten message, LET ME WERM MY WAY INTO YOUR HART.

We, the eleven members of GET HIM, could go on forever listing all the stuff he's done to us, but we've decided to list just thirteen things. The unlucky number, thirteen, is only the beginning.

From now on Matthew Martin is going to have to watch out. We're going to make his life as miserable as he has made ours. He's never going to know when something is going to happen.

WE ARE SERIOUS!!
WE ARE ANGRY!!
WE AREN'T GOING TO TAKE IT ANYMORE!!!!!!!!!!!!!!!!!!!!!!!!!!!!!!

SIGNED,

    VANESSA SINGER, President

    KATIE DELANEY, Vice President

    JIL! HUDSON, Secretary

    LIZZIE DORAN, Treasurer

MEMBERS: Cathy Atwood, Lisa Levine, Jessica Weeks, Zoe Alexander, Chloe Fulton, Ryma Browne, and Sarah Montgomery

Vanessa Singer

Katie Delaney

Jill Hudson

Lizzie Doran

Cathy Atwood   Lisa Levine

Sarah Montgomery   Jessica Weeks

Ryma Browne

Zoe Alexander

Chapter 12

"You're in for it," Joshua says, when the boys discover the GET HIM declaration on Matthew's desk. "I'm glad that I'm not you."

"Me too," says Tyler White. "But then I'm always glad that I'm not you. I'm glad I'm not you when we're playing Keepaway. I'm glad I'm not you when we're opening up our lunches. I'm glad—"

"Shut up," Matthew says.

Tyler continues, "And I'm really glad that I'm not you today. When all the girls gang up on someone, it's awful."

Matthew looks at the declaration that has been stuck to his desk with plastic imitation dog do and then he looks up at Tyler again. "Shut up."

"Really original." Tyler smiles at him.

"You only wish you were me when we're playing with the computer or Nintendo." Matthew stares at him.

Tyler stares back, but he's the first one to blink and look away.

Matthew smiles for the first time since he's gotten into the classroom and seen what's on his desk.

All of the boys in the class are crowding around his desk.

All of the girls are standing by the aquarium, talking to each other and looking his way.

Some of the girls are giggling.

Others are glaring.

Vanessa Singer looks very proud of herself.

Matthew looks around the classroom and tries to figure out what to do next.

The girls keep glaring and giggling.

Matthew is in deep trouble and he knows it.

He's not going to let anyone else know that he knows it.

Mrs. Stanton walks into the room and looks around.

Everyone tries to look very innocent. They immediately head for their desks, very quietly.

Mrs. Stanton looks around, trying to figure out what's going on without making too big a deal of it.

She looks at Matthew, who she figures has probably done something.

He is putting away the incriminating evidence, the plastic dog do and the declaration.

It's going right into his backpack.

There's no way that he's going to be a squealer.

That just isn't done in the sixth grade at E.E.E.

It's okay to tell on a brother or sister at home but not to tell on a classmate at school, as long as it's not a serious thing, the kind of thing that kids really should tell grown-ups.

This is not a serious thing. It's serious, but not SERI-OUS, like drugs or abuse or something dangerous.

There's no way that he's going to act like a baby and have Mrs. Stanton take care of it by talking to the girls. That would only make things worse, and Matthew Martin has a feeling that things are going to be bad enough as it is.

Vanessa Singer keeps sneaking looks at him and snickering.

"Would you like to share the joke with us, Vanessa, dear?" Mrs. Stanton says stuff like that a lot when she wants kids to stop fooling around.

It works.

Vanessa takes her notebook out of her desk and looks at the next spelling list.

So does everyone else.

There is a lot of giggling going around.

Not just the girls, but the boys too.

All of the boys but Matthew, who is beginning to wonder if he's finally going to be paid back for all the things he has done to other people.

Matthew goes into his desk and takes out his spelling list.

Someone has put Saran Wrap over all the stuff in his

desk and covered the wrap with lime Jell-O. It keeps wiggling back and forth.

It looks so gross.

Matthew wishes he had thought of doing it . . . to someone else, probably to Vanessa Singer. But he would have added little pieces of his mother's tofu, which would have made it look really gross.

But he didn't think of it. Someone else did and now it was in Matthew's desk, looking like the Slime That Ate Califon.

Green Jell-O was the only flavor he hated. Someone who knew his habits was out to get him.

Looking around the room, he realized that there were eleven someones who were out to get him.

This wasn't fair to do to someone with a birthday coming up, someone who was going to be very busy getting ready for his party, someone who didn't want to waste his time thinking about what a bunch of dumb girls were going to do to him.

Maybe this will be it, Matthew thinks. Maybe the dumb girls have had their dumb fun and they'll leave me alone.

Three minutes later Matthew feels someone kicking the bottom of his chair.

He turns around to check it out.

It's Lizzie Doran . . . and she's smiling.

Chapter 13

"Matthew. Something seems to be bothering you lately."
Mr. Martin looks up from the book he is reading.

"It's nothing." Matthew shakes his head and continues
to doodle all over his math homework.

"Are you sure?" Mr. Martin stares at his son. "You
know you can tell me anything. And now is a good time,
with your mother and your sister out shopping for an
outfit for the dance."

Matthew draws a skull and crossbones on the paper
and labels it POIZON: FOR SIXTH-GRADE GIRLS.
"No. No trouble at all."

He looks down at the paper and thinks about how rotten everything has been lately, how all the girls are making his life absolutely miserable, how most of the other boys don't want to start an anti-girl club, how even Joshua won't do it, and how Joshua had said, "The girls aren't against all of us, just you. And, Matthew, you've got to admit it, they do have reasons to be mad at you."

Matthew thinks about all of the stuff he's done to the girls, but he also thinks about how he's done stuff to everyone. It's not that he's especially against the girls, it's just that school gets so boring sometimes that he's got to do something to liven it up. He thinks about how all of the girls have been against him for three days now, kicking his seat, putting signs on his back saying things like SO DUMB HE SPELLS IT DUM and GET HIM WANTS YOU TO KICK HIM. He thinks about how someone's putting messages into the computer saying things like MATTHEW MARTIN IS NOT USER FRIENDLY and WATCH OUT . . . WE'RE GOING TO PUT A MAGNET NEXT TO ALL YOUR DISKS AND WIPE THEM OUT, and how Jil! Hudson has been doing really terrible things like telling everyone that they are engaged and that he is secretly going steady with her, then, after she says that, she makes these disgusting barfing noises and all of the girls giggle.

"Son. Are you sure you're all right? You haven't mentioned your party once today. Your mother and I are getting a little concerned." Mr. Martin puts down his book.

Shaking his head, Matthew says, "It's all right, Pop. Honest."

All right, Matthew thinks. Ha! All right. There are eleven people picking on me. It's not fair. So, it's true.

Sometimes I do things to other people, but I don't mean to be really mean. I don't gang up on anyone, and I have eleven people against me all at once. But what's the use of telling anyone?

"Matthew." Mr. Martin stands up. "I've been thinking. As one of your birthday presents, your mother and I were going to give you a bubble-making set, with instructions for making huge bubbles, for doing lots of tricks. Why don't you and I take that present out now and try some stuff out so that you can use it at your birthday party?"

Matthew smiles. Finally.

Mr. Martin says, "I'll go get the bubbles. Don't follow me. I don't want you to know where the secret hiding place is."

As his father leaves, Matthew smiles again.

He knows where the secret hiding place is, where all the secret hiding places are.

After all, when a person has spent his entire life living in one house, it's easy to figure out stuff like that, unless, of course, you are a prince or princess and live in a huge castle. There are probably millions of places in a castle to hide things, but most people, Matthew is sure, live in places where anyone can figure out the hiding places after almost eleven years of life. And Matthew has figured them out.

Sometimes stuff is hidden in the old trunk in the attic. Sometimes, if it's small enough, it's in his mother's drawer where she keeps her nightgowns. Sometimes it's in the garage, hidden behind the rakes and stuff, where the parents are sure no kid is going to look. Once, at Christmas, they even hid stuff in boxes in the freezer.

Since his mother had labeled it LIVER, Matthew never found it.

Matthew is sure that the bubble stuff is on the top shelf of his father's closet, behind the scarves.

He sneaks into his parents' bedroom and spies on his father, who is taking the present out of the clothes hamper in the bathroom.

Wrong, Matthew thinks, but at least I know another hiding place.

Matthew quietly rushes back into the living room, jumping on the couch and landing in a horizontal position. He stares up at the ceiling as if he's been lying there for hours.

Carrying the package into the living room, Mr. Martin says, "We'd better do this outside. Your mother's going to have a cow if we get soap all over the furniture."

As they head outside Matthew thinks about some of the weird stuff his parents say.

His father is always saying "Your mother's going to have a cow if . . ." When Matthew was little he used to wonder where they were going to put the cow if his mother actually had it. He always hoped that it would go into Amanda's room, where it would sleep in her bed and keep her awake all night mooing. But his mother never did have a cow, even if she did get pretty angry sometimes.

In the front yard Matthew and his father pour the bubble mixture into a large aluminum baking pan and then make large wands, using coat hangers with string wrapped around them.

The bubbles are huge.

Matthew only wishes he could make them big enough

to put a dumb sixth-grade girl inside each one and float them all up to Mars, or at least over Califon River, so that some bird could peck the bubbles and the girls would plop into the water.

Just as Matthew starts to say something one of Mr. Martin's bubbles travels across the lawn and lands on Matthew, breaking right on his face.

"YUG." The taste of the bubbles is not wonderful, nor is the sticky feeling all over his face.

Mr. Martin starts to laugh and moves closer, blowing more bubbles at Matthew, using a smaller wand.

This is war.

Matthew runs over to the box, takes out another small wand, and starts blowing bubbles into his father's face.

His father is winning until Matthew gets a lot of liquid into the wand and blows so hard that there's no bubble, just liquid glob all over his father's face.

This is more than war. It's annihilation.

Mr. Martin grabs his son's foot, pulls him to the ground, and sits on him.

Then he takes the wand and keeps blowing bubbles all over Matthew's face.

Matthew can't stop laughing.

He also can't manage to get the wand away from his father.

"Boys." Mrs. Martin arrives on the scene.

Amanda is right behind her. "You two are so gross."

Mr. Martin blows bubbles toward her. "I am not gross. I am your father."

"Mother. Make them stop. Everyone can see them. What if one of my friends comes by?" Amanda sighs. "It's bad enough that my brother is so immature. . . ."

"Young lady. You better stop before you say anything else." Mr. Martin continues to blow bubbles at her and then starts blowing them at his wife. He is still sitting on his son.

"Stop. You're getting me all sticky." Mrs. Martin is laughing.

"You ain't seen nothing yet." Mr. Martin gets off his son and starts moving toward his wife. He's picked up the very large wand.

Mrs. Martin moves toward the faucet where the garden hose is attached.

"I'm getting out of here." Amanda clutches the packages containing her new clothes and runs into the house. "You are all nuts!"

"Nuts? We're your parents, not nuts," Mr. Martin tells his daughter and then turns back to Mrs. Martin. "Come here, my little cashew."

Matthew watches as his mother holds up the hose and says, "Michael Martin. I'm warning you. I've known you since second grade and there are days I don't think you've changed that much since then. If you blow bubbles at me once more, you're going to be sorry. Very sorry."

"I dare you." Mr. Martin grins, moves closer, and blows bubbles at her.

She aims the hose at her husband and turns the water on.

Soaked, he drops the bubbles and runs over to try to capture the hose.

Amanda sticks her head out the window. "Would you all stop? Please, you are so embarrassing."

Matthew watches as his mother continues to spray his

father until his father captures the hose and sprays his mother.

Amanda, in the background, is pleading for her parents to stop.

Soaked, Mr. and Mrs. Martin look at each other and laugh.

Then they hug each other, kiss, and then whisper something to each other.

Matthew is standing there, watching the whole thing.

After they whisper, his father hands the hose to Mrs. Martin and starts walking over to Matthew.

Both parents are grinning.

Matthew can tell he's going to get it.

As he tries to run, his father catches up and pulls him down to the ground again.

His mother rushes over with the hose, sprays Matthew, and then sprays Mr. Martin again.

The three of them are laughing.

Mrs. Martin looks down at the two very wet men in her family and says, "Maybe you guys should go take a nap right now and say a little prayer, like 'Now I spray me down to sleep.'"

Mr. Martin groans at the pun.

Matthew says, "I think we should buy a water bed."

Mr. Martin stands and reaches his hand down to help his son get up.

Mrs. Martin turns off the hose.

Matthew gets up.

His mother hugs him.

He hugs her back.

He's beginning to feel like the old Matthew, before the girls ganged up on him.

Amanda sticks her head out the window again. "Would you all come into the house? Please."

"Join us." Mr. Martin uses a funny, teasing voice.

Looking at her family as if she thinks they should all check into a Roach Motel, Amanda shakes her head and vanishes into the house.

Mrs. Martin says, "Inside, before we catch pneumonia."

As they squish their way back inside, Matthew thinks about how this has been the best day in a very long time, how those dumb girls have driven him nuts long enough, how the old Matthew is back again.

Those dumb girls better watch out.

Instead of GET HIM, it's going to be GET THEM.

GIRLS EASY TO TORMENT HOPES EVIL MATTHEW.

Chapter **14**

Matthew grins as he finishes printing up the list.

It may not be perfect. There may be more tortures to think of doing, but it's a start.

And there are thirteen on the list. Just like there were on the dumb girls' list.

Matthew is sure that the girls are going to regret the day that he started this war.

Leaving the computer on because he plans to get back to it once he gets a little snack, Matthew puts the printout next to the computer and heads for the kitchen.

WAYS TO GET EVEN

By Matthew Martin

1.

Put Silly Putty in Cathy Atwood's baloney sandwich.

2.

Next time Lizzie Doran kicks the back of my chair, grab her foot and not let go of it. Also, pretend to be looking under my chair for something and tie her laces together so that when she stands up, she won't be able to walk.

3.

Take the large science magnet and see if it can attach to all the girls who wear braces.

4.

Put a whoopie cushion on Vanessa Singer's chair.

5.

Make puking noises in Lisa Levine's ear. It always makes her sick.

6.

Since Sarah Montgomery has a horse, act like she smells like one. Say things like "Howdy, NEIGHbor." Sniff when I am near her, saying, "Hay. What did you step in?"

7.

Next time Jil! Hudson says that we are going to get married, tell her that the only one dum enough to marry her would be King Kong because he's a big ape just like she is.

8.

Tell Jimmy Sutherland, the fifth-grader that Chloe has a crush on, that she has the creeping crud.

Stand behind Zoe Alexander and ask, "What goes one
hundred miles an hour backwards?" and then blow my
snot back up my nose. That always gets her.

Pretend to take my eyeball out of my face and into
my mouth and wash it. That grosses out all the girls.

Put a sign on Vanessa Singer's desk. YOU CAN PICK
YOUR FRIENDS . . . YOU CAN PICK YOUR NOSE . . . BUT
VANESSA SINGER PICKS HER FRIEND'S NOSE.

When Katie Delaney is in front of the class giving
a book report, make faces at her, like trying to touch
my nose with my tongue, pulling my lower eyelids as
low as they can go, wiggling my ears. Katie busts a
gut when stuff like that happens. Do all of that
without getting caught by Mrs. Stanton.

Collect belly-button lint and toe crud from all of the
boys and put it in Vanessa Singer's desk.

Amanda and his mother are already there, doing something at the table.

Going over to see what's going on, Matthew looks at his mother putting artificial nails on top of Amanda's bitten-down fingernails.

The make-believe nails are bright red, and Amanda keeps grinning. .

"These look so wonderful," she gushes. "I'm going to look so grown-up for the dance."

She looks up at Matthew and says, "What are you staring at, nerd face?"

Matthew does not like being called "nerd face," especially when he has done nothing to deserve it.

He pretends to study Amanda's face. "How grown-up can you look when you have that giant ugly gross pimple on your chin? It looks like a volcano."

Quickly covering her chin with her hand, Amanda's whole mood changes. "Oh, no. What am I going to do? There are only two more days until the dance. I can't go. Mom, you have to call Danny and tell him that I have appendicitis."

"It's only a disgusting-looking pimple." Matthew smiles at her. "Maybe he gets turned on by pus."

"Matthew Martin. I want you to stop teasing your sister immediately." Mrs. Martin shakes her fist at him and then turns to her daughter. "Amanda. There is no pimple on your face. You have to stop letting your brother torment you like this."

Amanda rushes out of the kitchen to look in a mirror.

Matthew goes over to the refrigerator, opens the door, and asks, "Anything good to eat?"

Mrs. Martin says, "Matthew. This fighting has got to

stop. I'm sick and tired of the way you tease your sister all the time."

" 'Nerd face.' She called me 'nerd face,' " Matthew reminds her. "I didn't even do anything and she called me 'nerd face.' Do you think that was right?"

Mrs. Martin sighs and sits down at the table.

Amanda rushes back into the room. "You little nerd face. There was nothing on my face."

"Yes, there is." Matthew grins at her. "There is something on your face. Lopsided glasses."

"Matthew." Mrs. Martin stands up again. "Enough, and stop calling your brother 'nerd face,' Amanda."

Amanda smiles.

That is not the response that Matthew expects.

She also holds up the computer printout that Matthew has left in the study.

That is definitely not something that Matthew expected either.

"Mom. I just found something you really should look at." Amanda is trying hard to look concerned, not incredibly happy at getting back at her brother. "This could get dear little Matthew into big trouble at school. I would never show it to you if I weren't so worried."

Ha, Matthew thinks. Worried is not the right word.

Amanda continues, faking a very grown-up voice. "As I said, I'm only showing this to you because I don't want Matthew to do these things at school and maybe turn into a juvenile delinquent and maybe someday turn to a life of crime. It's for his own good, and I only hope that he doesn't use this opportunity to make up stories about things that he wants to make you believe that I've done."

Mrs. Martin stares at her children, not positive about the best way to handle the situation.

She wants to respect her children's privacy.

She also wants to protect them from harm.

She remembers all the times her own mother said, "Just wait until you have children of your own."

Amanda waves the list in front of her. "I'm serious. This could cause a lot of trouble and torture."

Mrs. Martin sighs again. "Amanda. Give me the list and then go to your room. I will finish helping you with your nails later."

Amanda smirks as she leaves the room.

Matthew watches as his mother reads the list.

Mrs. Martin turns away from him so that he can't see her face.

Matthew wonders if he can convince his mother that he is just doing homework that Mrs. Stanton assigned.

It's doubtful.

Mrs. Martin turns back and looks at her son.

Matthew can tell by her face that even though she's trying very hard not to smile, she's not going to accept any kidding around about this, that he's going to have to explain what's really going on.

Matthew sits down to, as his father says, face the music.

He only hopes that when everything is over, his parents won't cancel the sleep-over and that the only music that he will have to face is the guys singing "Happy Birthday to You."

Chapter 15

"Matthew, I'm willing to accept this essay as proof of your intention to not wage war with the girls of GET HIM." Mr. Martin keeps smiling, even though he is trying to look very strict. "You will, as I understand it, give up all thoughts of GET THEM. Correct?"

"Yeah." Matthew looks at the floor.

"Yeah?" Mr. Martin lifts his son's chin. "Yeah? Is that the way to talk while you are trying to convince your old man of the sincerity of your words? Look at me and tell me that you mean what you say."

WHY I WILL NOT TRY TO GET EVEN
BY MATTHEW MARTIN

I will not get even for many reasons.

The first one is that my parents say that if I do I can't have my birthday party. That is really the biggest reason that I won't try to get even.

I will also not try to get even because my parents will make me write another composition just like this one. I personally don't think it's a good idea to make a kid like me write something that's not for school, just for his parents. It's especially not grate (great) when the kid is not a good speller and they have said that everything should be spelled correctly. I personally believe that there should be a seperation (separation) between home and school.

My mother told me why I should not get even so I will use some of her reasons so that this paper is long enough. She said that even though some of the things seemed harm— less, someone could get hurt with some of them, if not fisically (phisically, physically), their feelings could get hurt. She also said that swallowing Silly Putty could be danjerus (dangerous), that braces are expensive to repair, and that I seem to have an abnormel (abnormil, abnormal) interest in snot.

I could tell that she wasn't _so_ mad, because there were times when she almost laughed out loud. But then she said how I should try to work things out more directly, maybe apologize for some of the things that had made the girls mad in the first place, and not ever do them again.

I tried to explain why that wasn't going to work (my mother doesn't realize what a crudball Vanessa Singer really is and how stubborn she can be). But I did agree to write this paper about how I won't do any of the things that I said I would do on my list.

So now that I have written this, I can have my party, right?

Signed,

Matthew Martin

"Yes, sir." Matthew sighs and looks his father in the eyes.

His father is smiling and remembering some of the things that he, himself, did when he was a kid. He is also remembering how his parents made him promise to do things that he really didn't want to do and only hopes that Matthew will really do what he has said that he would do. Disciplining his children is not one of Mr. Martin's favorite things about being a father.

Mr. Martin ruffles his son's hair. "Okay, your mother and I spoke to Mrs. Stanton this afternoon and she has promised to talk to the girls."

"Aw, Pop. You know I didn't want you to do that. Now everyone is going to think I'm a nerd, a complete and total nerd. Now the girls will really torture me and you've made me promise to do nothing. I'm a dead duck."

"It'll be all right," Mr. Martin says, hoping that it will be but not sure.

Fat chance, Matthew thinks. Mrs. Stanton will tell the dumb girls that they will get detention if they do something at school, but she can't control what they do off school grounds.

Matthew is sure that he is in deep, deep, deep, deep trouble. And there is nothing he can do about it since he's promised not to fight with the girls and to do nothing to Amanda for squealing on him.

Life sure isn't fair, Matthew thinks.

He's just glad that Amanda is out shopping with their mother so that she can't gloat about his problems.

He hopes that Danny Cohen regains his sanity and

un-asks her to the dance and that Amanda turns into a total social reject.

He tries to figure out what he can do to get back at all of the girls who are making his life miserable, but it's no use. His parents have warned him, if he breaks his promises, he will have *no* more birthday parties, not ever, no allowance, and two pounds of alfalfa sprouts and tofu a day. (The threat of alfalfa sprouts and tofu came from his father. His mother said, "Your father is just kidding about that. We don't use food as a reward or punishment.") Matthew heard his father mumble that sprouts weren't just punishment, they were torture.

Torture, Matthew knows, is what the girls are going to do to him when they realize that he can't fight back.

"Matthew. Where are you? Are you daydreaming?" his father asks.

Matthew looks up. "It's more of a nightmare."

"How about putting the tent up? That way if there are any problems with it, we'll know about them now instead of tomorrow, when everyone is here for the party. And it'll get your mind off your troubles."

"Great idea," Matthew says. "Also, I should probably fill the goody bags tonight and sample the candy to make sure that we aren't giving away any stale old candy. We wouldn't want anyone to get sick and sue us for a million billion dollars."

Putting his hand on his son's shoulder, Mr. Martin says, "I think it's my responsibility as your father to help you test that candy, especially the M&M's and the licorice, which are my personal all-time favorites."

"It's a deal." Matthew smiles, glad that his father is not as nutty about health food as his mother.

"Race you to the garage." His father starts running. "People over thirty get a head start."

Matthew and his father race to the garage to get the tent and to pig out on candy.

It's Matthew's last day as a ten-year-old and he intends to live it up.

Chapter 16

"Mom. Do you promise that you aren't going to have one of those goofy people from work come over here and embarrass me? All of the guys are going to think it's so corny to have people in costumes singing and dancing and acting like goofballs." Matthew moves his finger around the mixing bowl and picks up leftover icing.

"I promise." Mrs. Martin looks up from the cake that she's decorating. "It costs too much, even with my discount, and, anyway, everyone is booked this weekend. Also, I promised your sister not to do it since she is afraid that she, too, will die of embarrassment. I wonder when I turned into such an embarrassment for my children. Back in the old days, you used to think I was always right, always wonderful. . . . Look, I promise. I'm not sending anything . . . Girl Scouts' honor. . . ."

"You're not a Girl Scout," Matthew reminds her.

"Okay . . . mother's honor . . . wife's honor . . . working woman's honor."

"Mom!" Amanda calls out from her room.

"I'll be right there, honey." Mrs. Martin puts down the cake-decorating tube.

"Mom." Matthew looks at her. "This isn't fair. You keep going into Amanda's room to help her instead of getting ready for *my* party, which is definitely much more important. The guys are going to be here any minute, any minute and my cake only says Happy B. It's no fair. Amanda has been getting dressed for her stupid date for the last five hours. She keeps changing her clothes. She keeps trying on new makeup. She keeps practicing trying to walk without her glasses. She keeps tripping over things and looking squinty. She's really a mess. And you keep going in to help her."

"You have a first date only once." Mrs. Martin smiles. "Matthew, someday you will go out on your first date, and you'll care about how you look too."

Matthew picks up the cake-decorating tube, holds it over his face, and squeezes some icing into his mouth. Some of it spills onto his cheek. He wipes it off, streaking it across his face.

"On second thought, maybe you won't ever care." Mrs. Martin kisses him on the forehead.

"No licking it off my face." Matthew grins.

Mrs. Martin sighs. "Matthew."

"Mom!" Amanda yells. "It's an emergency. I can't decide which earrings to wear."

"Coming, honey." Mrs. Martin heads upstairs.

"Coming, honey." Matthew softly mimics his mother. "Coming, honey. Of course your stupid first date is very important, more important than my only son's birthday because . . . because you are such a dweeble that no one is ever going to ask you out again."

Matthew looks down at the cake, then up at the clock, and thinks that the guys could arrive anytime now. No one waits until the exact second the invitation says to show up. What if the guys show up and look at the cake and see only HAPPY B? They'll know that everyone in the family thinks that dumb Amanda is more important than he is.

Matthew points the decorating tube at the cake and thinks, Here goes. I can do this myself.

On the cake appear the words HAPPY BERTHDAY.

Matthew is very proud of himself for taking care of things.

He looks at the cake.

Something does not look right.

Matthew looks at it for a few minutes, but he isn't sure.

Amanda rushes into the kitchen, goes to the refrigerator, and pulls out a can of diet soda. "I'm never going to get ready on time."

"You've been getting ready for weeks. I don't understand what your problem is. Anyway, I've got problems of my own." Matthew points to the cake.

Amanda looks it. "Let me guess. You wrote out HAPPY BERTHDAY yourself."

"Mom did half of it, and then she had to go help you." Matthew makes a face.

Amanda debates leaving the cake the way it is, but then thinks about how rotten Matthew is going to feel if everyone sees how BIRTHDAY is misspelled. "It's I, not E. Look, is there any more icing left, besides what is on your face?"

Matthew hands her the mixing bowl.

Amanda looks at the clock on the wall, thinks about how she should be getting her nails on, and looks back at Matthew.

It is not going to be much fun for him if all his friends tease him on his birthday.

Taking a knife out of the drawer, Amanda scrapes the E off the cake, fills in the hole with brown carob icing, and inserts the I.

"All better now." Amanda grins at her brother. "Happy birthday, creepling. Now I've got to go."

She rushes out of the kitchen and back to her bedroom, where her mother is putting clothes back on hangers and placing them back in the closet.

Matthew looks at his cake and smiles.

Amanda did a pretty good job.

Nobody is going to be reminded what a lousy speller he is.

Amanda was actually nice for a change.

There was a good chance that this party was going to be great, especially if everyone brings terrific presents, Matthew thinks.

The doorbell rings.

It's Joshua, carrying a sleeping bag and a present.

The present looks very flat, not like a toy or game or computer disk or anything good at all.

Joshua hands the present to him. "It's a dumb shirt. My mother made me bring it. I wanted to get you a Destroyers of the Earth zap gun, but my mother said your mother wouldn't allow it in the house."

"I wish you had brought it. I could have used it on the girls of GET HIM." Matthew holds up the present and pretends that it is a zap gun.

In walks Mr. Martin, carrying a bag. "Hi, guys. Ice-cream delivery."

"What flavor did you get? Did you get my favorite one? Bubble Gum Ripple?" Joshua asks.

Shaking his head, Mr. Martin says, "No. That was the last flavor of the month. I got Double Fudge with Butterscotch, Blueberry Cheesecake . . ."

"Yuk," say both of the boys at the same time.

"More of it for me." Mr. Martin rubs his stomach. "It's not often that we get real ice cream into this house. So when we do I try to make the most of it. We also have Peanut Brickle, Pistachio, Chocolate Mint, and Banana Royale."

"That's enough for an army." Joshua licks his lips.

Mrs. Martin comes back into the kitchen and looks at all of the ice cream that Mr. Martin is showing the boys.

"All that sugar." She sighs. "We're going to have a group of boys spending the night with us who are all sugared up. I thought that you were going to get one flavor, maybe two."

Mr. Martin tries to look sorry for what he has done, but it's obvious that he's not. "They didn't have Granola

Grape or Sprout Sundae as this month's flavor of the month."

Mrs. Martin shakes her head. "I married you for better or for worse. Your food preferences are definitely not among your better qualities."

As Mr. Martin puts the ice cream into the refrigerator, the doorbell rings.

Billy Kellerman and Pablo Martinez arrive.

Mrs. Martin goes outside to talk to Mrs. Kellerman.

Earlier in the week Mrs. Martin had Matthew give all the boys a paper to take home. A parent was to fill out the form, saying whether the boy was allergic to anything, who to call in case of emergency, and if a boy got homesick, was he to go home or stay anyway.

Mrs. Martin believes in organization.

Billy Kellerman never takes papers home.

Tyler White and Mark Ellison show up on their bikes, doing wheelies.

Brian Bruno, Patrick Ryan, and David Cohen march up to the front door, with their sleeping bags on their heads, singing "I Love a Parade."

"Let the wild rumpus begin!" yells Joshua, using a saying from one of his favorite books from when he was a little kid.

Everyone goes into the den.

Matthew opens the presents.

There are more baseball cards for his collection and a new Nintendo cartridge, a couple of tapes, a magic set, a squirting calculator, the shirt that Joshua's mother picked out, a Transformer that turns into a working camera (a present sent by Matthew's grandmother in Florida), The

Oozone Layer, a game that gets slime all over everyone, and more clothes, picked out by more mothers.

"Awesome," "Rad," and "Excellent" are some of the responses as Matthew opens the package from Mark El-lison and Patrick Ryan.

In the package are suction-cup bullet holes, to be put on someone's skin. Also included are capsules of make-believe blood, to be broken over the skin where the bul-let holes are placed.

Matthew looks over at his mother as he unwraps some more of the items in the box.

She definitely looks underwhelmed by the presents.

Matthew only hopes that she will let him keep these gifts.

There are also some make-believe tattoos and one of those baseballs that look like a monster's eye.

"Wow. Thanks." Matthew puts the eyeball in front of his own eyeball.

His mother is shaking her head.

His father is laughing.

"I can use this all for my next book report." Matthew thinks fast. "Mrs. Stanton said we should do a mystery. This stuff will come in handy for the oral report."

"I'm sure." Mrs. Martin sounds a little sarcastic.

"Really." Matthew puts on his most angelic look and decides to change the subject and not to pull out the last item, a skull-and-crossbones bike sticker. "What's in that big box over there?"

Mr. and Mrs. Martin hand Matthew a large package.

Matthew rips off the wrapping paper as his mother yells, "Save the bow. We can use it again."

Matthew forgets and demolishes the bow, opening the package to discover a remote-control car.

"Luck–y," say several of the guys at the same time.

"Let me see that." Tyler holds out his hands.

"Me first." Matthew takes the car out of the box and he and his father set it up.

"This is from your sister." Mrs. Martin shows Matthew a certificate that says that Matthew now has a subscription to *Radio Control Car Action.*

"Luck–y."

"I get first dibs on borrowing it after you're done," Joshua says.

Mr. and Mrs. Martin go out of the room and some of the guys start playing with the car.

Two tournaments begin. Nintendo and Computer.

Four people play.

The rest cheer or boo.

Soon everyone goes over to the bowl of Gummy Worms and puts a Gummy Worm above his lips, pretending to be the principal, Mr. Curtis, who has just started to grow a mustache.

The doorbell rings.

"I thought everyone was here already," Matthew says, eating the tail of the Gummy Worm, or maybe it's the head. He's not sure.

"I think it's my brother, my stepbrother," David says.

"The date," Joshua says. "Let's do something to get them all embarrassed."

"My brother said he would kill me if we did anything." David shakes his head. "Let's not and say we did. That way I'll still be alive to have my own birthday party in two months."

Matthew is glad that David has said not to do anything, that he isn't the one who had to do it.

He's thinking about how, even though Amanda is a real pain sometimes, she did help him with the birthday cake and she really doesn't deserve to have her first date messed up, even though it would, in some ways, be a lot of fun to do something to her.

"You guys promise to stay in here, and I'll ask my mom if we can have the cake and ice cream now."

"A bribe. I'll take it," Brian Bruno says.

Mark Ellison, who has ten Gummy Worms coming out of his mouth, is walking around shaking his head at everyone so that the worms look like they are alive.

Matthew goes out of the room and sees Amanda standing in the hallway. She's trying to keep her balance on her new high heels, biting her press-on nails, and attempting to see without her glasses.

She's a wreck.

Matthew tries to make Amanda feel better. "For a goofy girl, you don't look half bad."

Amanda smiles, a little. "Thank you . . . I think."

They walk into the living room.

Mr. and Mrs. Martin are standing there talking to Danny, who looks a little nervous too.

Mr. Martin takes out a camera and says, "I hope that you two don't mind, but I'd love to take a picture."

"Oh, Daddy, that's so embarrassing." Amanda looks like she's going to die.

Danny says, "If you're going to take a picture of anything, sir, I think you might want to take a picture of what's happening on your sidewalk."

"What's happening?" Mr. and Mrs. Martin immediately go to the front door.

So does Amanda, who says, "This is so gross." She starts to giggle.

Matthew goes up to the door and looks out.

It's the girls of GET HIM and they are marching back and forth, carrying picket signs and wearing T-shirts that they have decorated themselves.

The T-shirts say:

The girls of GET HIM strike again!

Chapter **17**

"Oh, gross. This is so gross." Amanda is laughing.

"They asked me to bring in a message." Danny is laughing, too, although he's also feeling a little embarrassed that there are so many people around to watch him pick up his date. "They said that they're willing to negotiate a settlement. All that it will take is an apology in front of the whole class."

"Apologize for what?" Matthew fails to see the humor in the situation.

"For just about everything, apparently." Danny is

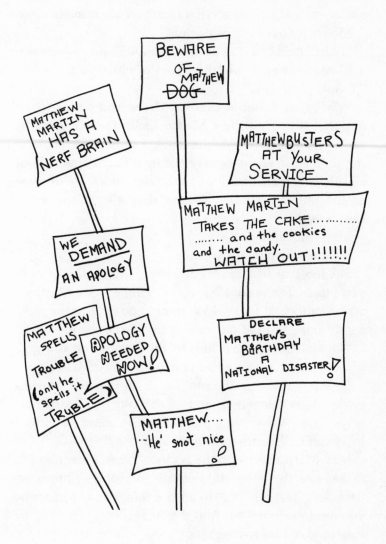

having a lot of trouble not smiling. David has told him about some of the things that Matthew has done in class.

Matthew looks at his parents.

"Matthew. How do you spell trouble?" his father asks.

Closing his eyes, Matthew tries to visualize the word. "T–R–U–B–B–L–E."

"Well, that poster is wrong." Mr. Martin points to the one that says "Matthew Martin spells Trouble, only he spells it TRUBLE." "Maybe that's a symbol for some of the problems. The girls may not be totally correct about all things, but they may be on the right track about some of the things. Don't you think that it's time to work things out?"

Mrs. Martin nods.

Danny whispers to Amanda.

She looks at her parents and says, "Mom. Dad. Could you please do the *Leave It to Beaver* number with Matthew after Danny and I leave? We have to go over to the Jacksons' house and get our ride to the dance there."

"Okay, Wally. We'll talk to the Beav after you go." Mr. Martin is laughing and pretending to be Mr. Cleaver.

Leave It to Beaver is the old TV show that the Martins always watch together, and at the end Mr. Martin always says "Why can't our family be more like that? Why can't all families be more like that?"

Mrs. Martin gets into the act too. "Now, I want you to make sure that you children are careful, get home on time, and 'Just Say No' to all the things that you know you are to say 'no' to. And if you see Eddie Haskell, be sure to give him my regards."

Mrs. Martin always hisses when Eddie Haskell comes on the show.

Amanda looks at Danny. "I can't help it. My family is weird. I warned you."

"That's all right. Ever since my mother's remarriage, my family tries to be *The Brady Bunch.*" Danny reaches out and holds Amanda's hand. "It could be worse. They could try to be *The Munsters.*"

As Amanda and Danny go out the door, the girls all start yelling things like "MATTHEW MARTIN COME OUT RIGHT NOW! WE DEMAND AN APOLOGY. APOLOGIZE. APOLOGIZE. APOLOGIZE."

Amanda turns around and looks at Matthew. "Thank you so much for causing all of this commotion when all I want to do is have a happy memory of this."

"It's not my fault." Matthew goes to the door.

"It's always your fault." Amanda trips on her high heels.

Danny catches her.

The girls catch sight of Matthew at the door. "APOL-OGIZE. APOLOGIZE. APOLOGIZE. APOLOGIZE."

"What are you going to do?" Joshua walks into the living room.

The rest of the boys follow.

Tyler White waves to Zoe Alexander, who is his girl-friend.

Cupping his hands, he calls out, "I thought you were going over to Vanessa's to have a pajama party!"

She calls back, "We are, but first this."

Vanessa Singer looks very proud of herself.

Matthew wishes that a tornado would come and take all of the girls to Kansas.

The tornado doesn't materialize.

"I think you should talk to them before the neighbors begin to complain about the noise," Mr. Martin says.

"Let them complain." Matthew shakes his head. "Then they'll call the cops and have the girls arrested."

"I think that there is a better solution." Mrs. Martin puts her hand on her son's shoulder.

"Call the FBI in?" Matthew feels that would be the better solution.

"Matthew," Mrs. Martin says.

"I think you should apologize and let the girls have ice cream and cake with us," Joshua suggests.

"No way." Matthew shakes his head.

Pablo Martinez says, "Come on, Matthew. The girls aren't so bad. You know that you like some of them, that you used to be friends with them."

Matthew thinks about how hard it is to always be the youngest one in his class, how he always feels like he's playing Catch-Up, how it seems like everyone is always a little ahead of him. Can he help it that he's always the youngest? In his family. In his class.

He wishes that some new younger kid would move into town and be put in the sixth-grade class.

He wishes that his parents would have another kid, a younger one, obviously.

He wonders if it's too late to ask for one, instead of the remote-control car.

He wonders if he can have both, the baby brother and the remote-control car.

"Matthew. You've got to do something." Billy Kellerman points to the girls, who are now sitting on the lawn with their arms linked, singing an old peace song that

Mrs. Stanton taught them in history class, "We Shall Overcome."

Matthew looks out at the girls and then turns back and says, "Let's just ignore them."

"Ignoring the problem won't make it go away," Mrs. Martin says.

"My mother always says that too." Mark Ellison nods.

"My parents too," say a couple of the other kids.

"Everyone else's parents would let them ignore the girls." Matthew is feeling desperate.

"Matthew. Let me list all the possible responses to that." Mr. Martin is smiling. " 'Would we let you jump off the roof if everyone else's parents did?' 'We're not everyone else's parents.' 'As long as you are living under our roof, it doesn't matter what other people's parents say.' And that old standby, 'No way, José.' Now, did I miss any?"

"My father always says 'I brought you into this world. I can take you out,' " Billy Kellerman offers.

Mr. Martin says, "So you see, Matthew, my son, you are going to have to deal with this problem. Think of your friends waiting for their ice cream and cake. Think of your dad waiting for his ice cream and cake. Think of how much better you're going to feel once you resolve this problem."

Looking at the boys, then at his parents, and then out the window at the girls, Matthew realizes there's only one thing to do (actually two, if you count moving to Disneyland, which his parents probably would not let him do). So there really is only one thing to do. Talk to the girls and work out some kind of truce.

"Okay, I'll talk to them," Matthew says softly.

"Terrific. I'll get a pillowcase, tie it to a stick, and go out to the enemy camp to work out the arrangements. That's what they always do in movies and books." Mr. Martin heads out of the room.

"Honey, I don't think that's necessary," Mrs. Martin calls after him.

"It'll be fun," he calls back.

Mrs. Martin looks at Matthew and smiles. "Your father. I married him because of his high sense of play. He sometimes drives me nuts with his high sense of play, and you take after him."

Everyone watches as Mr. Martin heads out the door.

Everyone watches as Mr. Martin goes over to the group of singing girls, sits down with them, and talks.

The talk goes on for several minutes.

Finally, Mr. Martin returns and says to Matthew, "Here's the deal. You are very lucky, young man, that you have a lawyer for a father. This is what I have negotiated. The girls will come inside. You will apologize for all the things that you did that led to the formation of GET HIM, and I want that apology to sound sincere."

"Okay." Matthew stares at the floor.

"And," Mr. Martin continues, "the girls have agreed, if your apology sounds sincere, to apologize for all the things that led to the formation of GET THEM."

"Okay." That word sounds a lot happier this time when Matthew says it.

"And," Mr. Martin says, "the last part of the negotiations involved the kind of cake to be served. One of the demands is that there be no carob icing, just mocha, and that the cake be filled with butterscotch custard. That was their final demand. I gave in to it in the cause of furthering trust and understanding."

"Huh." Mrs. Martin puts her hands on her hips. "There's something fishy going on here. That is *your* favorite cake."

"Not fishy—cakey." Mr. Martin puts his hand on his son's head. "What say we wrap up the apology session, and I'll make the supreme sacrifice and run over to the supermarket and get the cake."

Matthew smiles at his father, realizing that his troubles are almost over. "It's a deal."

Chapter **18**

"First you had to eat crow, then you got to eat cake." Mr. Martin pats his son's back.

"Huh?" Matthew looks up at his father.

"Eating crow is a phrase that means you had to say you were sorry in such a way that it seemed like a major punishment." Sounding like a teacher, Mr. Martin reaches for his third piece of cake.

"It would have been easier to eat a crow than to look at Vanessa acting like such a big-shot winner." Matthew runs his finger around the paper at the edge of the cake to get the icing.

The male Martins are in the kitchen alone while the party is going on in the living room.

Mrs. Martin is hiding out in her bedroom, reading a book and worrying about the health of her family.

"Actually, things turned out all right," Mr. Martin says. "The girls did apologize too. Although I do think that Vanessa saying 'I'm sorry that it was necessary to do all those things to you' was not the best apology in the world. But look at the bright side, there's a truce and you are the host of the first sixth-grade girl-boy party. And you are a year older."

"And I got lots of great presents." Matthew grins.

Mr. Martin grins back. "You really did. Do you think I could borrow the suction-cup bullet holes and one of the capsules of make-believe blood? I'd like to wear them to work on Monday."

"Absolutely." Matthew nods.

"Thanks, kid." Mr. Martin wipes his face off. "Are all the crumbs gone? I don't want any evidence when I go back to the room. Otherwise, your mom is going to say . . ."

Both male Martins, in unison, say, "Lips that touch sugar won't touch mine."

Matthew heads into the living room.

The compact disk player is on, loud.

Most of the girls are standing on one side of the room.

The boys are on the other.

Walking up to Matthew, Vanessa Singer points at him and whispers, "Listen, doofball. No more silly stuff or the girls of GET HIM will activate Plan B."

Matthew debates doing something really gross, like another SBD or belching out a chorus of "Happy

Birthday." Instead, he clutches his heart and pretends to writhe in pain. "Oh, no. Not Plan B. Anything but Plan B."

Sticking his tongue out, he crosses his eyes and sinks to the floor, muttering, "Help. She's picking on me. What's Plan B?"

Vanessa looks down at him. Then she looks at everyone else looking at them and realizes that they know that she is the one who started it this time.

She sticks her nose up in the air and, after stepping over Matthew, says loudly, "Just remember, a truce is a truce."

Matthew jumps up and calls out, "And a moose is a moose!"

Everyone laughs, except Vanessa.

Then Matthew goes over to Joshua and says, "I guess there's no chance for the tournaments to finish."

"I don't see why not." Joshua cups his hands and calls out, "Nintendo and Computer tournaments are back on. Who else wants to join up?"

"Also, we can drive the remote-control car," Tyler says, turning to Zoe and smiling. "Want to go for a ride with me?"

"But you don't have your license." Zoe frowns.

"It's a miniature car," Lisa Levine tells her.

"And it's remote," says Jil! Hudson, who thinks that Zoe is a little remote too.

"Anywhere you want to go, I want to go, too, Tyler," says Zoe, sounding like syrup.

Ryma Browne pretends to stick her finger in her mouth and makes little retching noises.

"Someday, when you two are more mature, you will

understand what it's like to have a boyfriend." Zoe makes a face at Jil! and Ryma.

"Trust me. I will never act the way you do around boys." Ryma makes a face.

"My mother told me how to act and she must be right. I have the boyfriend, not you." Zoe looks like she owns the world.

Jil! debates asking if Zoe's mother knows so much about men, how come she has had three husbands, but she decides not to.

Tyler looks a little embarrassed, but he also looks like he enjoys the attention. With four older brothers, he thinks he knows a lot about dating.

The tournaments begin.

Billy Kellerman wins at Nintendo.

His prize is a hand-held game called Parachute.

Matthew wins at Computer, but since it's his party, the prize goes to the second-prize winner, Chloe Fulton.

"Good game," Matthew says, glad that he had practiced for a week before the party and extra glad that Chloe didn't know which game would be used in the tournament.

Chloe gets a set of science-fiction books, which is terrific since she loves to read everything, especially science fiction.

"Can I borrow them when you're done?" Pablo Martinez asks.

"Absolutely."

By the time the boy-girl part of the party is almost over, everyone is talking to everyone else. No one is fighting. Nobody is making a big deal out of it being a boy-girl party, except for Zoe, who keeps blowing into

Tyler's ear because she heard that was a sexy thing to do. He keeps wiping the spit off, finally begging, "Say it. Don't spray it."

Jil! Hudson comes up to Matthew when he is standing alone by the bowl of Gummy Worms. "I'm really sorry that I teased you so much about being boyfriend and girlfriend. I was just joking around."

Matthew looks at Jil!, who is nervously chewing on the ends of her hair.

He thinks about how much fun she can be when she isn't picking on him, how she's always thinking of fun things to do, how she's always so creative. He also thinks about Zoe's comment about how Jil! isn't mature enough to have a boyfriend.

"That's okay." He grins. "Someday, when you're more grown-up, maybe then we can be boyfriend and girlfriend. And if you really play your cards right, maybe we could be just like the Cleavers and live happily ever after."

Then he picks up a Gummy Worm and puts it above his lip to form a mustache.

Chapter 19

Sunday.

All the boys have finally left after the sleep-over.

Two barfed.

All of them watched as Danny and Amanda came back from their date.

All of them made kissing sounds with their lips on their hands when Danny started to kiss Amanda as they stood on the porch.

Amanda threatened to put all of them in the microwave, piece by piece, and then she begged to be sent away to boarding school or to have Matthew sent to reform school.

Matthew said it was not his fault.

Amanda disagreed.

The boys, at breakfast, ate ninety-four pancakes, spilled the syrup all over the floor, devoured three packages of vegetarian sausage without realizing that it wasn't the real thing, drank two containers of orange juice, and then held a belching contest.

Mrs. Martin refused to award a prize to the winner of that competition.

"Thank goodness for paper plates," Mr. Martin says, throwing a bunch of them into the garbage.

Trying to fit just one more glass into the dishwasher, Mrs. Martin said, "I didn't get any sleep last night with all of the laughing, did you?"

Mr. Martin shakes his head.

"What did the boys want to talk to you about this morning? What was so private?" she asks, starting the dishwasher.

"They wanted me to judge the joke-telling competition." Mr. Martin looks in the freezer to see if there is any ice cream left over for breakfast.

He can't find any.

"Who won?" Mrs. Martin closes the freezer door before he can find out that she has hidden the ice-cream container in the lettuce crisper container. "And what was the joke?"

"Patrick Ryan. And you don't want to know." Mr. Martin sits down at the table.

Matthew enters the kitchen very quietly, whispering, "Is the coast clear? Did Amanda go over to Cindy's or is

she hiding behind the refrigerator waiting for the chance
to kill me?"

"She left an hour ago." Mr. Martin shakes his head.
"You know, you and the guys should not have used the
computer to make up that sign, Amanda Martin makes a
Spectacle(s) out of herself. That wasn't very nice, and,
anyway, how did you know that glasses used to be called
spectacles?"

"We studied Ben Franklin." Matthew is glad that he
can show his parents that he actually remembers something from school.

There's silence at the table for a few minutes while
Matthew waits to see if his parents are going to say anything else about how he's always tormenting Amanda.

Mr. and Mrs. Martin say nothing. They are so glad
that there is peace and quiet again in their house.

"Mom." Matthew breaks the silence. "Dad. Do you
realize that there are only three hundred and sixty-four
days, eight hours, and twenty-eight minutes until my
next birthday?"

Mr. and Mrs. Martin look at each other as if they have
been put in front of a firing squad.

Mrs. Martin is the first to speak. "Matthew Martin.
Everyone else's children said they wouldn't bother their
parents this morning. What do you have to say about
that?"

Matthew grins. "I'm not everyone else's child."

"True." Mr. Martin looks at his son and realizes that
Matthew has the suction-cup bullet holes on his arms.
"Very true."

The looks that his parents give each other are unmis-
takable.

What will Matthew do next?

PAULA DANZIGER has often been asked to write a book with a boy as the main character, and she has finally done it! Her three nephews provide her with a wealth of material, and her nine-year-old nephew Sam, "the consultant," has been a special help and inspiration.

Ms. Danziger is the author of several best-selling novels for young people, including *Remember Me to Harold Square, This Place Has No Atmosphere, It's an Aardvark-Eat-Turtle World, The Divorce Express, Can You Sue Your Parents for Malpractice?, There's a Bat in Bunk Five, The Pistachio Prescription,* and *The Cat Ate My Gymsuit.*

Ms. Danziger lives in New York City and Bearsville, New York.